LETHE

BRIAN DAFFERN

BHD Publishing

To My Loving Wife, Karen
Thank you for always supporting my dreams

CHAPTER ONE

The wiry, black-furred creature crept across the arid desert; its beady red eyes fixed on a sixteen-year-old boy somewhere ahead. Its sharp pointed claws dug into the sand with each step, crushing small rodents and lizards in its path. With a mighty leap, it cleared the low ridge separating them and opened its long snout to take in the scents of the area, leading it to the boy like an internal compass. It could almost taste victory as it started running faster, determined to find him no matter who or what was standing in its way.

The wind hissed across the parched desert sands and the barren brush of the open range, stirring up small whirlwinds of dust that swept along with a rolling tumbleweed or two. A soft rustling broke the stillness in the otherwise silent night, and a figure stirred in the pale moonlight.

A young teen lay sprawled on the hard ground in nothing but an oversized hospital gown, its white fabric-stained brown by dirt and dried sweat. He opened gritty eyes and yawned a dry-mouthed yawn as he slowly rose. His muscles ached from lack of use, and he stretched them out with a deep, rumbling groan.

Taking in his unfamiliar surroundings, the boy was puzzled to find himself alone in the middle of nowhere. Mountains reared up on either side of him, their rocky faces jutting into the star-strewn sky, and he noticed strange cacti dotted all around him like sentinels; but to the south, there appeared to be nothing more than vast emptiness.

He wiped away a layer of sand that had gathered atop his head while he slept and felt a coldness run through him when he realized what had happened: someone had shaved his head bald. He scratched it curiously as he tried to process where he was and how he'd gotten here.

The boy looked around in disbelief; the desert was endless and silent. His bare feet carefully placed each step as he squinted against the darkness. He noticed a sharp rock and cursed his misfortune as it stabbed him in the heel with its jagged edges. He grabbed his injured foot, hopping on the other one until the pain dulled before releasing it to the ground and kicking away the offending stone.

He realized now that he wasn't wearing shoes or clothes, just a light hospital gown that covered him down to his knees, held closed by two small ties across the top and bottom of his back. He quickly checked the ties, ensuring they were securely fastened so his bare bottom would not be exposed to this lonely world.

"Where am I?" he cried out into the desert, though he knew no one would answer him. He closed his eyes and tried to remember how he came to be here, but all he could recall was a blank void.

The questions kept spinning around in his head, and as he accepted that he had no answers to them, a greater dread settled over him. Not only did he not remember where he was or how he got there, but he couldn't even remember his name.

Then, a random thought appeared in his mind, triggered by a half-forgotten movie with hospital scenes. He remembered that they put identification bands on the patients' wrists in the film, and suddenly feeling hopeful, he looked down at his wrists. A thin white band was coiled loosely around his left one.

Gripping it tightly between two fingers, he raised it close to his eyes and tried to make out what was written on it in the moonlight. After a few moments of adjusting, he could make out the one word printed across it: Duncan.

He turned it over several times, looking for any other details, but those six letters covered its surface. Was this really his name? Even though something inside him said no, it was as good as anything else at his current disposal.

A chill ran up his spine, and the air suddenly thickened around him. His heart raced like a runaway train, pounding in his chest as fear crawled up from within. Summoning every ounce of courage, Duncan cautiously stepped out into the night, peering left and right for any danger lurking in the shadows. He walked faster, willing himself forward over the rocky terrain, his eyes darting to every crevice and crack for signs of pursuit. Something was coming for him somewhere in the darkness beyond; he could feel it. He couldn't be sure who or what it was, but whatever it was didn't bring good tidings. Despite feeling overwhelmed by dread, a sense of curiosity coursed through him--what would this mysterious pursuer want with him?

CHAPTER TWO

The gorilla-sized beast prowled across the sand until it stopped at a spot where the boy's scent should have been. He snorted and twitched his nostrils but found nothing. His ears perked up as he sensed movement behind him, but when he turned around, there was nothing there. Frustration boiled within him like a volcano about to erupt.

Then he spotted it - a tiny bloody rock. He knew with absolute certainty that it belonged to the boy. The creature's frenzy began to build, and he paced in a circle, eyes fixed on the moon above.

But as much as he tried, he could not detect the boy's scent. The olfactory senses of the creature were failing it; it had never faced this problem before. It began to wonder if it had lost the boy forever. Every deep breath of air brought more sand into its nose, making things worse.

Determined to find the boy, he located the nearest rock formation. He efficiently ran towards the higher ground, using its mighty arms and opposable thumbs to grip tightly onto rocky ledges.

Finally arriving at the top, he squatted and scanned the area below. No movement caught his eye. No sound reached his ears. He sniffed multiple times and could only smell sand.

He blew short, controlled breaths to clear out the dust collected in his nose caused by all the snorting in the sand. The creature would do anything to get its hands on that boy. But thoughts of losing or not finding the boy filled him with rage that was hard to control.

Duncan's breath quickened, and he felt his heart beating faster as he walked hurriedly through the light brown landscape. The pitch-black sky glittered with stars, giving off just enough light to see by, and in the distance, he could make out faint artificial lights high in the sky – probable streetlamps of some sort. His feet burned to break into a run towards the inviting light, but the sharp rock he had encountered earlier warned him against it.

CRUNCH! CRUNCH! CRUNCH!

Duncan stopped and spun around. Something was moving amongst the dead brush on his left side. "Who's there?" he asked warily, studying the large, wilted bushes. Frozen with fear, his legs too stiff to run, he watched as the dead vegetation began to shake quickly from side to side, then abruptly parted.

The boy held his breath as a shape pushed through the underbrush. His heart raced, and his mouth went dry as he waited for what could be a giant, monstrous creature to step out of the shadows. But instead of a monster, a medium-sized coyote emerged, its fur blacker than any canine Duncan had ever remembered. Its red eyes shone with hunger and curiosity as it entered the clearing. It's thin belly and bony legs betrayed that it hadn't eaten in a while.

Duncan shouted and waved his arms in a desperate attempt to scare off the animal, but the coyote only cocked its head to the side, confused by the display. It cautiously took another few steps forward, its tongue rolling out of its salivating mouth. His fear was replaced by anger and determination not to become dinner for this scavenger.

He picked up a palm-sized rock and threw it at the animal's feet, but the coyote only glanced down at it and then back up at him, its hungry gaze intensifying with defiance. He searched for another rock. He realized from the corner of his eye that the coyote had stepped closer to him when he wasn't looking directly at it.

The boy retreated step by step, but the coyote had already outmaneuvered him. Two more approached from his left, growling with sharp teeth bared, while another pair closed in on his right with low snarls that filled the air. Five wolves, all starving, surrounded him. They didn't let hunger cloud their judgment - this boy was their prey.

In terror, Duncan knew he was done for. A single coyote had been a manageable nuisance to chase away. But five? He braced himself for the inevitable attack, feeling as if his end was near.

Then a sound, a howl unlike anything he'd ever heard, pierced the night air. The tone alone sent shivers of fear and horror through him. The coyotes were equally affected by the mysterious noise. They sniffed around cautiously, tails between their legs, before suddenly turning tail and fleeing back into the brush they came from. Duncan could hear soft whines echoing around him, but at least he was safe now. What could have possibly scared off the hungry pack?

The boy's heart raced as he heard a second chilling howl come from behind him, and he knew it could only be one of two possibilities: either the coyotes had changed their minds and were coming back, or something much worse was after him. He dug his heels into the sand and sprinted southward, glancing over his shoulder every few seconds to check for movement.

The mysterious creature's third howl echoed eerily through the desert air, followed by an abrupt eruption of barking from the five coyotes. Fearful that whatever had made that fierce howling might be heading toward him, Duncan picked up his pace even more. There were several painful yelps in succession before all went quiet.

He strained his eyes, looking for any sign of life, desperate for a safe hiding place. Eventually, he spotted a faint glow on the horizon. It was lights from a small distant gas station. He ran even faster, pushing himself beyond exhaustion until he finally reached the gas station. Its carport was lined with lightbulbs and sheltered a few medium-sized gas pumps next to a ten-table diner. He could hear voices coming from inside, indicating safety in numbers.

Duncan walked with purpose, his heart thumping in anticipation. His footsteps echoed off the cold asphalt as he approached the flickering neon sign that promised help. He kept his eyes on the distant horizon, wary of any movement, while grappling with the notion that whatever had killed the coyotes was coming for him too.

He arrived at the diner and slowly approached the stairs that led up to the entrance door. He stopped at the door, turning to take one last look around before entering. The desert was eerily quiet, with no whisper stirring in the winds. He felt relieved but apprehensive; whatever was out there could still find him if he stayed here too long.

There was a forest of dying trees on a hill behind the diner. It could provide a good hiding spot. Should he keep moving or go in? He was tired and hungry and knew he couldn't get too far without resting or eating. His decision was made. Gripping the handle firmly, Duncan pushed open the door and stepped into the warm light of the diner.

CHAPTER THREE

Twenty mutilated bodies lay scattered in the moon-drenched streets, some with glassy eyes still wide open in shock, some missing limbs torn from their torsos. A black sedan crept cautiously along the deserted dirt road, weaving around the corpses and occasionally stopping for Agent Brian Trudy to peer curiously at each one.

He stopped in front of one of the buildings that lined the road and stepped out of his vehicle. He was a tall man with robust features and obsidian hair concealed beneath a crisp black suit. His right shoulder held a slight bulge, where his Berretta handgun was tucked away. He surveyed the street with weary blue eyes before speaking to himself in a low murmur. "At least they weren't civilians."

Making his way inside the saloon, Agent Trudy pushed through the wooden bat wing doors and felt a thick dust cloud settle over him as he entered. The darkness was only punctured by a lantern blazing in the far corner near an old window, where an elderly man with scarred features sat at a dusty table with a filthy glass clasped firmly in his hands.

"General," Agent Trudy said warmly as he extended his hand.

The scar-faced man took Trudy's hand firmly and motioned for the agent to sit down. Trudy nervously surveyed his surroundings before cautiously lowering himself into the chair. His eyes darted to the General's movements as he slipped his hand into his jacket and gripped the butt of his revolver.

"We're alone," the General said, his voice low and raspy. "Relax. Now, tell me. What was so important that we had to meet in person?"

"It's close to the deadline, and I've been reading your status logs." Trudy tensed, wary of the General's reaction. "You're not making satisfactory progress on developing Biological Weapons of Mass Destruction. The BWMDs are supposed to be delivered in two weeks, and the only thing filling your logs is notes about this cloning business."

"It is equally important work," the General defended. "Do you realize that when they cloned that sheep in 1997, they had to try 277 times to get it right? I got it right on the third time."

"That may be impressive, but that isn't why your team was pulled from Stem Cell research after the President's announcement," Agent Trudy argued, struggling to keep his temper in check despite growing frustration with their lack of progress. "We need these weapons for immediate deployment to help our troops stationed throughout the Middle East. We agreed that you would have them ready by now, yet here we are with nothing but excuses."

"I do so hate acronyms and abbreviations. It makes it seem as if the work is not valid. If you ask about it, please use its proper name - Biological Weapons of Mass Destruction," the General countered gruffly.

"Really? Do you want to argue over semantics? Did you hear anything I said?"

"I do happen to follow the news," the General replied coolly. "And I know the need for my creations. They will be ready on time with more features than you requested."

"More features? More what exactly?"

"Not only cloning and creating mixed breeds of animals but resurrecting the dead! My research team has somehow managed to clone the gene responsible for immortality!"

"Really," Trudy said skeptically. "Is that why there are all those men in the street? Are they part of your preparations for this resurrection process?"

The General leaned forward, his gaze cold and hard. "Don't insult my intelligence. They are part of my Blue Agent process. They were unfortunate casualties from a test of my strongest biological weapon."

"From the looks of them, it appears to have been successful. But if they're out there, where is this weapon?"

"We are currently in the middle of retrieving it from its hiding place in the desert. It was designed per your specifications; as with every other organism we create, it depends on a particular factor for survival. If removed, it dies. That is how we control our genetically engineered creations."

"And how does that get your creature back?"

"Our creature - as you call it - was intended to be dropped into enemy territory at night and wreak havoc until sunrise when it dies upon contact with light. Its skin contains keratin proteins that disintegrate upon exposure to sunrays, like a vampire in daylight."

Trudy's face was contorted in rage as he shouted, "You lost your most prized weapon, and your only plan to get it back is to let it burn up in sunlight! That's completely unacceptable."

The General remained composed and replied, "That's only our last resort. My men will have it back soon."

"Your men are dead?"

"I have more."

Trudy sneered at him, "What? How many more? You know what, never mind. If you have more of those clones, are you sure they will bring it back? Your 'men' can barely function as humans, and I hear they are masquerading as Federal Agents. Is that true?"

"A necessary ruse. Don't let that skew you from the success they are. I used the best DNA Somatic Cell Nuclear Transfer sequences available from the military donor subject," the General explained calmly, "The process creates an exact duplicate, and the intelligence has been the same. I can't explain it, but they carry the same instincts as their previous selves."

Trudy didn't want to argue any further with the arrogant General and stated firmly, "If you want to violate the NIH guidelines on cloning, then you do it, but not on our dime. We only pay you to violate their guidelines on manipulating the mixed breed DNA and give us our weapon."

The General gave Agent Trudy a piercing glare of disdain, silently requesting that he refrain from using abbreviations.

"Very well," Agent Trudy conceded, his voice rising angrily. "The National Institutes of Health guidelines – the government agency responsible for the expenditure of taxpayers' money on research projects. Happy? Now mark my words. If you don't deliver on time, we'll pull the plug. I'll be here two weeks from now to receive it. If this doesn't get done, I will drop you in a hole so deep that no one will be able to find you again."

He stood up and offered his hand to the General, who promptly slapped a journal into his palm.

"This is my latest status report. As you can see, it's mostly about your Biological Weapons of Mass Destruction."

"Excellent," Agent Trudy replied with a sneer before turning away without another word. He climbed into his car and rolled up the windows. Even though the temperature was sweltering, blocking the stench of decaying bodies from sickening him was more important. The blue agents' corpses may have been clones but they still had their unique stink of dead flesh.

Once he crossed the city limit and left the dead town behind him, Agent Trudy cracked open the windows and heard a distant and savage howl that chilled him to his bones. Could this be the creature he was waiting for? The delivery?

CHAPTER FOUR

Duncan eased open the door and peered inside. The diner was aglow from a single row of exposed light bulbs along the ceiling, revealing ten scruffy, unshaven men huddled around a television set mounted on the wall farthest away from him. As if the slam of the door's frame hadn't been enough to alert them, every head in the establishment spun towards Duncan when he stepped over the threshold.

The man in front of him, who looked like he'd just returned from a long shift at a coalmine, stared at him for an uncomfortably long moment before speaking. "You look like you've seen better days," he said gruffly. "What happened to you? Are you okay?"

Duncan shook his head and ran a hand across his dirty bald head. He could only imagine what they were thinking. His appearance was hardly typical - not even reminiscent of how he'd looked earlier that day.

"I don't know," he replied softly. "Coyotes have chased me, I think... I feel like I've been walking for hours, and someone seems to be following me."

The bearded man motioned for him to come further into the room and directed him to one of the empty booths. Several other patrons stood up, swapping worried glances as their friend walked off with Duncan in tow.

"My name is Gus," he said gruffly as they settled in at the booth. "This here is my station. How did you get way out here anyway?"

"I don't know." Duncan pinched the bridge of his nose and scratched his head with his free hand. He had no idea where this place was or how he got there - all he remembered was waking up alone in the middle of nowhere wearing nothing but a hospital gown. How could he express that and not sound nuts?

Gus stepped closer to the boy, and his nose crinkled at the smell of stale smoke that clung to him. "You kind of discovered that yourself in the desert, I guess," Gus said, looking down at the boy's dirt-covered feet.

"My feet are sore," Duncan replied in a soft voice.

An old man with pure white hair walked up beside Gus and suggested, "Maybe he fell out the back of an ambulance. I've heard of it happening before out in Washington County."

Gus shook his head. "You're an idiot, Frank. If he fell out, they would've picked him up. Besides, there aren't any roads out there. Just the main one that runs by this place. No, something else happened to him."

Duncan asked, "Is there anything I could eat? I don't have any way to pay for it, but I am starving."

Gus smiled. "There sure is. Frank, go get the boy some soup and grab Doug's overalls and boots out of the large gray locker while you're back there. They should fit him." Frank grumbled as he went around the cramped room and entered the kitchen through a door in the back.

"Thank you," Duncan said as Gus pulled up a chair and sat beside him in the booth.

"Doug is my boy. He's about your size," Gus said, nodding toward the door in the corner of the room. "It isn't much, but it should cover you up better than that open-backed dress you have on."

"It's a gown," Duncan corrected him softly.

"Sure, sorry," Gus said with a chuckle before asking Duncan his name. Duncan told him he couldn't remember anything - not even his name - and showed him the band around his arm with 'Duncan' printed on it.

"Well, until a better one comes along, Duncan it is. Who knows, if you can't remember anything, it could be your name."

The boy's hands were soiled and trembling as he nervously fiddled at the diner table, his eyes darting around the room. He felt a deep dread and terror as if something dark lurked out of sight. When Gus asked him if he remembered anything, his voice shook when he said, "There's something after me. I don't know what or who it is, but I know it's bad."

Gus nodded reassuringly and patted Duncan on the back. "Don't you worry none, boy? There's nothing out there that can get you in here. My boys and I will make darn sure that nothing happens to you. Won't we, boys?" A chorus of agreement replied from the scruffy-looking men around the table. He added, "I suppose you don't know who gave you that haircut either?"

Duncan ran his hand over his bare scalp embarrassedly. "No, I don't, Gus," he said softly. "But it sure feels funny."

A few moments later, Frank returned with a pair of overalls, boots, and a steaming bowl of chicken noodle soup.

Duncan began to devour the meal hungrily as Gus remarked with a smile, "It just isn't right to do that to a boy. Your hair should be allowed to grow and flow."

Duncan quickly agreed while continuing to savor every spoonful before him.

CLANG! CLANG! CLANG!

Out in the street, an ominous sound reverberated through the small diner. His eyes widened.

"What was that?" Frank asked, startled as his gaze flew to the men watching the game on the television. His friends all seemed unfazed.

"Boy, you're jumpy. It just sounded like the garbage cans around the side," Gus replied with a shrug. "Maybe a coyote is back there."

"I'll check," Frank said, stepping back into the kitchen and coming out a few seconds later, shotgun in hand and a wild gleam in his eyes. "I've been wanting to shoot something for a long time."

Duncan could feel the menace from outside and dropped his spoon into his near-empty bowl. "Don't go out there," he pleaded, his skin prickling with apprehension. "It feels awful."

Frank laughed heartily, missing teeth and eyes dancing with anticipation. "Don't worry, boy," he drawled, patting the shotgun affectionately.

"I have a mighty big gun that feels pretty bad, too. If anything is out there that isn't supposed to be. I'll take care of it."

Duncan watched him leave, fear freezing him to his seat as his mind raced back to a long night in the desert dodging howling coyotes and unknown predators.

Gus shook his head, breaking Duncan's trance. "Maybe you should get dressed," he said, nodding towards the uniform of overalls and boots. "Old Frank may not look like much, but he can take care of himself."

Duncan nodded mutely before getting up from his seat and grabbing his clothes.

"Just go all the way to the back, and the bathroom is the last door on the left. It has a bright red stop sign nailed to it. You can't miss it."

Duncan navigated through rows of tables and booths, past the group of chattering customers, into the kitchen, and towards the back of the diner. When he came upon the restroom, he noticed its door was askew with pieces of wood haphazardly nailed around it to keep it shut. He slowly inched open the creaky door and was met with a wall of smoke. Duncan stepped inside cautiously, wrinkling his nose at the musty smell in each corner of the room. He immediately noticed how outdated everything looked: The green-stained toilet seat had several tears, the shower curtain was ripped in multiple places, and a thick layer of dust and mold clung to each fixture.

He shut the door behind him and started getting dressed. Even when pushed all the way closed, something didn't feel secure about this door latch - every few seconds, it would inch open just enough that one could see Duncan standing there trying to change. He heaved a tired sigh before pushing it shut again and continued to dress.

"Who's winning?" Gus asked, joining his buddies in front of the Television set. He pulled up a metal chair, sat in it reversed, and stared at the basketball game playing out in front of them. After several minutes and a few bad plays rolled across the screen, Gus realized Frank hadn't returned. "I wonder what's taking Frank so darn long."

"Not sure," a tall thin man in a plaid shirt replied. "Don't care, either. Why don't you go see?"

"Yeah, Bill, I think I will. And you're going to come with me."

"Me?" Bill said, pointing at the screen while protesting against such injustice. "But...but I wanted to watch the game! Can you blame me for striving for some normalcy? I've been stuck in that damn factory for months?"

Gus nodded understandingly before replying, "Come on, Bill, or else I won't let you back in my restaurant for a month."

Bill groaned before reluctantly standing up from his chair and following Gus in Frank's direction. "He better be hurt, or I'll kill him."

Gus and Bill cautiously opened the door to the diner, both tensing at the sudden sound of a loud, terrified shriek emanating from around the side of the building. Gus started down the steps first, instinctively leaning his body out to get a better look. "I don't see him," he called over his shoulder. "That sounded like he was hurt. What do you think, Bill?"

Bill stepped back into the small restaurant with a shocked expression.

"What was that?" "Was that a scream?" Duncan asked, running back to the main room, and the rest of the men hurried to the entrance, his body already half-dressed in overalls.

"It sounded like Frank," Bill said grimly.

A chill ran through Duncan's whole body, and he felt a flush of panic wash over him. He had an inkling that something terrible was about to happen when Frank left earlier, and now it was coming true. "I knew it was bad," he muttered, fastening the final strap of his overalls across his bare right shoulder. "I just knew it. I told you he shouldn't go out there, and now look at what's happened."

Gus gave Duncan's shoulder a reassuring pat and spoke up with some forced bravado, "As far as we know, nothing's happened. Calm down." He addressed the rest of the men in the room, "Old Frank could have tripped or stepped in one of my Coyote traps. The boys and I will go check it out. You stay here."

Gus hooked his thumbs into the straps of his overalls and bellowed out a command, "Come on, boys! We need to check it out!"

The men paused as if frozen in time until Gus repeated himself more sternly. Reluctantly, they followed him outside, leaving Duncan alone in the restaurant, gripping tightly onto a table edge to steady his shaking body while watching anxiously from inside.

He went to the window. A few minutes had passed since they left, and all things were quiet. He was worried.

As if reading his mind, the men bolted around the corner of the building and ran towards the diner. They were pushing and nudging each other out of the way, each wanting to be in the pack's lead. A few stumbled but recovered quickly and continued their run toward the entrance. One by one, the big hairy men ran into the diner. Gus entered last and locked the door behind them.

The men fell to the floor, out of breath and gasping for air. It was apparent that none had exercised in years; sweat dripped down their faces, and their cheeks were red with exertion. Fear clouded their eyes as they tried to regain control of their labored breathing.

"What happened?" Duncan asked. "What did you see?"

"He's...he's...he's...he's dead," Bill stuttered. "Frank is dead."

Gus sat on a chair, feverishly hacking up phlegm as he pulled off his cap to wipe sweat from his forehead with a grubby handkerchief. He spit a wad of saliva to his left before turning to Duncan with a grave expression.

"What'd you say was after you, boy?" Bill asked, holding his chest and struggling for breath.

"I don't know."

"Well, whatever it is, it tore Frank up. His body was mangled — like an animal got at him or something."

Bill's eyes widened, and his breathing became labored as he scoured the room. "I mean torn up," he shouted. "Something clawed him to death, and it was something big. Half his face was missing, ripped apart, and most of his right arm had been shredded away. We found his hand still clinging to the shotgun."

Gus stepped forward, a deep frown creasing his forehead, and gestured for Bill to be silent. "That's enough. No need to scare the boy any further than he already is."

Bill shot him an incredulous look. "Scare him? Heck, Gus, I'm already scared! Why not him too? Whatever killed Frank is coming for him."

Gus shook his head and sighed heavily. "You don't know that. It could just be some enormous coyote or something."

"Or something," Bill replied skeptically. "We both know it wasn't no coyote. He was practically pulverized into pieces. And the thing that did it is coming for him." He looked around at the other men in the room and continued, his voice rising with desperation. "I say we throw him outside and let it be. At least we'll be safe. We don't even know him anyway. He just showed up here, and one of us is dead the next minute. Who knows, maybe he's in cahoots with whatever killed Frank? Throw him out before it's too late for us, right guys?"

The crowd of men murmured their agreement in hushed tones.

Gus put up his hands and cut them off midsentence. "We are not putting this boy out there," he said sternly, his gaze sweeping across each man individually until they nodded in acknowledgment and looked down shamefully. "Even if whatever killed Frank wanted him, we have a moral obligation to protect the kid. He asked us for help. What if it was one of your kids?"

Duncan piped up, speaking quietly but confidently in response to the words, "I don't remember my age either," he said, raising a small hand timidly, "but I'm old enough to know that I don't want to die."

Gus turned back to the group of men with a determined glint in his eye, refusing to give them another chance to speak against Duncan. "We will protect the boy," he declared firmly.

The men inside the diner jumped from their seats when a loud, echoing roar penetrated the room. They rushed to the windows, pressing against the glass with fear-filled eyes as they searched for any sign of movement outside. At first, nothing stirred in the darkness between the bright gas pumps and the front door, but then a rustle atop the carport caught their attention. In a seemingly choreographed dance, every light mounted above the pumps shattered one after another until all that remained was a deep inky blackness.

Bill's voice trembled as he spoke up, "You ever heard of a coyote that could do that? We're all going to die. Throw the boy out there before it's too late!"

Gus quickly shouted, "We will not throw the boy out there! Stop saying that, you hear?"

Duncan whimpered, "I don't want to die."

Standing in the diner's doorway, Gus motioned for Duncan to retreat. "I won't let you stay here and risk getting hurt. Why don't you take cover in the back, boy? The rest of us should be able to handle whatever's coming."

One of the other men pointed towards a dark shape looming closer. "I saw something out there – two big, red eyes watching us!" he exclaimed.

Gus's voice was firm but gentle as he spoke again. "Run, boy. Don't stop, no matter what you hear. We'll protect you."

Trembling, Duncan hugged him and ran across the diner and into the kitchen beyond. He heard glass shattering and several screams inside the restaurant as his feet pounded against the tile flooring. He wanted desperately to help, but he knew he wouldn't stand a chance if they couldn't handle it.

Duncan glanced around the kitchen frantically, his eyes darting from the bathroom in the corner to the metal freezer door next to it and the slightly open storeroom opposite. A small hallway ran towards the back of the room, and he dashed toward a door at the end. He yanked it open, squinting into the darkness. His heart felt like a lead weight as he noticed a flashlight on the floor beside him and scooped it up. He fumbled to switch it on, relieved when its beam shone across his trembling hand. "I'm sorry," he whispered, not looking back at the diner behind him. He took off, pumping his legs through an ascent up a sand dune before dropping into the forested gully beyond. The sounds of desperate screams followed him, impossibly loud with each shallow breath and tear that slipped down his face.

CHAPTER FIVE

Sheriff John McCoo stumbled away from the diner. His hand clamped over his nose and mouth. He gagged a few times as he moved further away, trying to distance himself from the awful smell that had assailed him as soon as he stepped inside. He paused, leaning against the squad car, catching his breath. Deputy David Johnson greeted him with a grim look on his face.

"It's a mess all right," Sheriff McCoo said between gasps for air. "Unbelievable - would be the word I think best describes it."

Deputy Johnson shook his head. "What happened, Sheriff? I heard a bear tore them apart."

The Sheriff smirked. "Not likely in the desert, and the woodland area back there is not that big."

Deputy Johnson scowled. "Maybe it escaped from a circus or something? That's only in the movies. And besides, any responsible circus would have reported their bear missing immediately to avoid lawsuits. No, this was something different."

"I guess," Deputy Johnson said with a shudder. "What else could it have been?"

The Sheriff shrugged. "Doc Williams is still inside – we'll wait to hear what he has to say and go from there."

The Deputy shifted uneasily, glancing nervously at the diner door before looking back at the Sheriff. "This will definitely kill the tourism we've been getting in town," he added with a weak smile.

Sheriff McCoo and his Deputy stood vigil outside the diner, their faces solemn. It had been a bloody scene inside the restaurant - bodies strewn across the floor like discarded dolls. The silence was punctuated by what could have only been desperate cries for help swiftly silenced as each person succumbed to their wounds.

The Doctor trudged out of the diner with a slight limp and signaled his assistants to follow suit. They rushed back towards the ambulance, their arms loaded with medical equipment and supplies. Meanwhile, Sheriff McCoo made his way up the steps and met Doctor Williams halfway. "Can he talk?" he asked, nodding towards the man on the stretcher carried out of the diner.

Doctor Wilbur Williams adjusted his glasses and leaned closer to examine the body. His two assistants quickly followed suit and rushed ahead of him, pushing the stretcher toward the ambulance. As they descended the stairs, something miraculous happened - a faint groan came from the body.

The Medical Examiner dropped to his knees beside the man on the stretcher. He fumbled through his bag until he found what he was looking for - a stethoscope. He placed it against the man's chest and smiled when he heard a faint but steady heart The Sheriff watched as Doc Williams and his team rushed the stretcher carrying Gus into the back of the ambulance. "Not now, John," Doc said in an urgent tone. "We have to get him to the hospital."

Sheriff McCoo gritted his teeth and clenched his jaw. He had to know what had happened to his friend. With no time for an argument, he quickly maneuvered around the stretcher, stopped it, crouched beside the motionless man, and grabbed his hand. The Sheriff leaned in close and implored Gus to open his eyes. "What did this?" he asked, desperate to glean some answers before it was too late.

Gus opened his blood-filled eyes slowly, and his head tilted until he could make out the blurry vision of Sheriff McCoo. He motioned for the Sheriff to lean in closer before whispering through a dry throat, "The boy... You have got to find the boy."

Before Sheriff McCoo could probe further, Gus lost consciousness, and his hand slipped from his grip. He shook it frantically, trying vainly to coax some sign of life from his friend. "Gus, wake up! What boy? What did you mean? You've got to tell me."

Just then, a voice spoke behind him, "I believe we can help explain what he meant."

Sheriff McCoo rose from his crouch and spun around. Standing before him were two men dressed identically in navy blue suits, white shirts, and blue ties. The only defining feature between them was their glasses; one pair clear, one dark black – they could have been twins.

The medical examiner rushed back to the diner, his heart pounding in anticipation. He could hear the distant sound of sirens coming from the parking lot and see a plume of dust as the ambulance carrying Gus drove away. Suddenly, three men in navy blue suits were in front of him. The first two had almost identical features.

In contrast, the third man stood taller than the others and had a stern expression. He reached into his pocket and flipped open a wallet with a badge across it. "FBI, Agent Lee. This is Agents Washington and Niche," he said gruffly, pointing at the men beside him. "We must ask that you or your men not enter the crime scene. Our people are coming, and we will be working the case."

Deputy Johnson stepped forward and began to protest but was quickly silenced by the Sheriff holding up his hand.

Agent Lee pulled out a 3x5 photo of the boy and spread it across the fold-out table in front of Sheriff McCoo. He pointed to each corner of the photo and said, "This is him. We've been on his tail for months, and he's managed to stay one step ahead of us. We know he's responsible for similar slaughters at locations across four states."

Sheriff McCoo stared down at the photo and scrutinized every detail before responding. He shook his head in disbelief, then asked, "What makes you think this boy is capable of such carnage? I mean, Gus seemed pretty out of it."

Agent Lee sucked in a deep breath and explained, "We can't be sure how he did it, but we know he was present at each scene. This is why we must find him. He's extremely dangerous."

The Sheriff pocketed the photo and declared that he'd distribute it among his deputies to keep an eye out for suspicious activity. He asked Agent Washington to accompany his medical examiner into the diner in case other survivors needed assistance. Agent Lee considered the offer and agreed. The vans pulled into the gas station, and the side doors opened in unison. Sheriff McCoo was shocked that the new arrivals were dressed identically in dark blue suits, too eerily similar to the three Federal Agents he had already met for it to be a coincidence.

The FBI men headed straight for the diner and filed inside. Moments later, Doctor Williams emerged, pulling off red-stained latex gloves from his hands and dropping them into a plastic bag beside the small staircase. He walked over to Sheriff McCoo and spoke gravely, "John, no more men are alive in there. Those guys didn't stand a chance. When I get them back to the hospital, I'll measure the cuts and bites to tell you what kind of animal it was. A human didn't do it."

Agent Lee stepped forward at these words, "You won't be examining the bodies, Doctor. We will be taking them to our facility."

Sheriff McCoo's brow furrowed as he asked, "What facility? There aren't any FBI installations or offices nearby."

Agent Lee's lips curled into a tight smile, and he shot the Sheriff and Doctor a sideways glance. The Sheriff's face was contorted in frustration, and the Doctor's jaw clenched as the Agent spoke. "Not that we need to explain ourselves, but we have a mobile unit close by that will serve the purpose."

The Doctor erupted angrily; his voice thundered as he shouted, "That's not right! As the local Medical Examiner, I should be involved."

The Sheriff tried to settle him down, reminding him of their jurisdiction laws and the importance of staying in the loop.

Agent Lee considered the men momentarily before acquiescing with a terse nod. He took a card from his coat pocket with his name and number and handed it to them. "We will publish our findings to both of you, and I am sure we will ask for your assistance in the future. This is my number if you need to reach me," he said, dripping with veiled innuendo. Agent Lee turned on his heels with one more fake smile and strode toward the diner entrance with the other Agents.

Not wanting to be left behind, the Sheriff and Doctor quickly followed up with their warning about safety, not that Agent Lee appeared to take much notice.

The Sheriff studied the Doctor, assessing his enthusiasm. His friend silently stared at him. He ran a hand through his salt-and-pepper hair and released a long sigh. "I'm not an idiot, Doc," he said. "I know. I want to return to the office and call to check this out. If I can verify what their task force is all about, then maybe I can find out what they are up to. I just can't imagine so many men searching for one little boy that can somehow kill all those men and make it look like an animal. Something is just not adding up."

The Deputy shifted uncomfortably on his feet, eager for something to do with this case. "What do you want me to do?"

"Nothing, David. And I mean it, nothing," the Sheriff replied sternly. He waited until the Deputy nodded in agreement before handing him a photo of a small bald boy with piercing blue eyes. "You can head back to the station and show this photo to the other men. Make sure they know to keep their eyes out for him."

The Deputy raised an eyebrow as he took the picture and peered at it curiously. "Why is he bald?"

The Sheriff rolled his eyes in exasperation and said, "How in the world do I know? Just do what I asked."

"Jeesh. Just asking," the Deputy muttered under his breath as he walked towards his car parked behind them in the parking lot. The engine roared to life a moment later, and he drove off, leaving behind a large cloud of dust as he left.

Once his Deputy was gone, Sheriff McCoo turned back to the Doctor and asked the question sitting on the tip of his tongue: "Are you sure that what we saw in there was done by an animal?"

"One hundred percent," the Doctor assured him as he glanced back at the dead lying nearby. "There is no way that anything human could make that kind of damage."

The Sheriff gave him a curt nod of thanks before turning away to head back to his car himself. "Thanks, Doc," he called over his shoulder as he opened his car door. "I will get back to you when I have some information. But until then, watch over Gus and let me know when he wakes up. I will send a deputy to the hospital to help keep watch."

"Why the extra guard? Do you think whatever did this will come back to finish off Gus?"

"Not at all. I am worried about the two-legged creatures we just dealt with. Something tells me these men will want everything and everyone connected with this, and I can't have them walking off with Gus."

CHAPTER SIX

Duncan trudged wearily through the desert, his feet aching from running for hours. He had managed to stay close to the road in case a car or truck should arrive, but the night was still, and no one passed. With the last of his energy, he kept putting one foot in front of the other, fighting off fear with each step.

When the first signs of dawn broke across the horizon, something inside Duncan warned that he would find safety in the brightness. Though he couldn't explain how he knew, he knew that monsters like his pursuer could not bear sunlight and could not focus their eyes in its glare.

His relief was palpable as he spotted a small shack ahead, nestled among bushes and cacti a hundred yards back from the road. Summoning the strength to put on an extra burst of speed, he made it to the hovel just as the sun rose. Duncan pushed the door to the shack and stepped inside, a hint of musty air lingering in his senses. His eyes settled on the piles of hay spread across the floor, and he smiled. The rustic shed was a home away from home, just what he needed to rest his head. He dropped to the ground, feeling the soft cushion of hay beneath him, and curled up in its bed. His body melted into exhaustion as a dream began to take him away.

Duncan found himself in an unfamiliar room with no windows, only one door, and complete darkness except for small beams of light shining beneath it. Hungry for the comfort of light, he called out for it but instead heard something else reply; a low growl that rumbled through the blackness like thunder. Duncan searched through the shadows, terror rising within him when two red eyes emerged from the night, watching him in the dark.

A deep laughter echoed from every corner of the darkness. It wasn't the creature. It sounded like an old man that smoked too much.

Choking back a scream, Duncan woke up suddenly with beads of sweat dripping down his forehead. He wiped them away with his sleeve.

Duncan opened the door of the small hut, and as soon as it was open, he felt a shock wave of heat and light from the harsh sun. He quickly stepped outside, finding himself in a sweltering heat different from any he had ever felt. His eyes protested against the whiteness that enveloped him, and he had to use his hand to shield them until they adjusted. He thought about the creature chasing him and, for a moment, imagined what it must have felt like to be in the same situation, blinded by light. As his vision cleared, he saw the road ahead winding its way southward, and it became clear that whether he was being pursued or not, the south was his only option.

He felt depleted but forced himself forward, hoping someone would stop their car so he could hitch a ride. Cars raced past him on either side of the road, ignoring his frantic arm waving as he begged for someone to pick him up. In desperation, he considered an even more dangerous idea, standing in the middle of the street so that any car passing would have to stop. But then Duncan heard a faint voice inside his head warning him of danger and begging him not to take such risks. It was true; his feet were already raw after walking through rough terrain the night before, and his overalls were soaked with sweat, making each step harder than before. He knew he couldn't make it much further without a ride.

Duncan squinted into the horizon, a shimmer of heat rising above the desert sand. The mist shimmered and shifted like water. Suddenly his eyes widened in anticipation as he watched the speck on the horizon grow more significant--a white van racing toward him. He dashed into the street and began waving his arms frantically, desperate for the vehicle to notice him. The van seemed too slow when it neared, and he could see the bright red light flashing from its roof. As it pulled off onto the shoulder, he heard its siren's wail cut through the desert air's stillness.

The driver leaned his head out of the ambulance window and shouted, "Do you need help, son?"

Duncan ducked his head and mumbled, "Yes, please. I'm stuck out here and have been walking forever. I need a ride if that's okay."

The driver eyed him skeptically and replied, "How did you get here with no one around? You don't look old enough to drive."

Duncan sighed in frustration as he admitted, "I got lost. Can I catch a ride into town with you? I need to get out of this heat."

The driver ran a hand over his grizzled face before reluctantly replying, "It's against protocol, but I can't leave you out here in this baking sun. Hop in."

With relief, Duncan raced around to the other side of the ambulance, jumped inside, and buckled up.

The sirens blared with urgency as the driver sped down the highway. He glanced at Duncan with an edge of concern and warned him to watch out for dehydration and see a doctor when they reached town.

As the ambulance pulled from the scene, Duncan leaned to his left and peered inside. He could see a bandaged man on a stretcher with a clear bag hanging above his head. A second paramedic checked the bag while he spoke to the driver. Duncan began to shake as he tried to understand what they were saying. Questions ran through his mind: What happened? Where did you find him? He was terrified of the answers but felt compelled to know.

The driver turned around before answering Duncan's questions, "He was attacked by some animal at the Gas and Eat dinner. He was the only one who survived."

The words hit Duncan like a punch in the gut, and tears spilled from his eyes. Without hesitation, he undid his seatbelt and made for the back of the ambulance. The driver yelled out for Lou, the other paramedic, to watch out for him as he scrambled over medical supplies and reached out for the patient. Lou stopped him halfway as he pleaded for them to let him see his friend. Finally, when it became too much for Duncan, he crumbled onto Lou's chest, desperately trying not to cry.

The paramedic grabbed the boy's arm, firmly steering him away from the stretcher and towards the entrance of the ambulance bay. Duncan trembled as he tried to protest, but his words were muffled by fear. The paramedic thought momentarily, then stepped back and released his grip on the child.

Duncan rushed forward, his heart pounding in his chest as he gazed at the lifeless figure before him. He whimpered, and tears streamed down his cheeks as he recognized his friend Gus, who lay pale and motionless. With trembling hands, Duncan reached out to touch his friend's face and was greeted with a faint gasp.

Gus' eyes flickered open, searching for Duncan in the shadows of the ambulance bay. "Is that you, Duncan?" His voice struggled to be heard above the sirens and passing vehicles outside.

"Yes," Duncan replied. He knelt beside Gus, brushing away strands of unruly hair plastered onto his forehead by sweat.

Gus's lips moved slowly as he spoke, barely audible over the whirring of medical machines nearby. "You got away...good. You have to keep moving. Don't stop. It won't." His voice trailed off as he lost consciousness once again.

Duncan leaned closer to Gus, screaming his name until he felt a hand on his shoulder.

The paramedic stood behind him - reassurance in his calm blue eyes. "It's okay, kid," he said softly. "He's just lost a lot of blood, but we've stopped the worst of it."

A wave of relief swept through Duncan as he released the muscle tension and rose to his feet.

"What did he say to you? What did he mean that something is after you? Does it have to do with how he was hurt?"

"I'm not sure," Duncan lied as his stomach tightened into a knot. "I guess I should get back up front. I wouldn't want you guys getting in trouble."

"Yeah, okay. Get on up there."

Duncan returned to the cab and fastened his seat belt around his waist. The knowledge that the injured man would be all right brought him comfort, but it was quickly replaced by heavy guilt for being involved at all.

"So, what did that guy say to you back there," the driver asked, glancing over at Duncan curiously.

"Oh, nothing," Duncan lied as fear crept up his spine again. "He just mumbled some crazy talk. I'm sure it was the medicine."

"Yeah, you're probably right. Now stay seated there. I don't want you going back there again."

"Sure," Duncan replied quietly, searching the passing scenery for an answer to Gus's warning. He knew he would eventually have to confront the monster no matter how far they drove or where he hid.

CHAPTER SEVEN

The ambulance screeched to a stop in front of the hospital, and the driver jumped down to help unload Gus from the back. The man's pale skin was tinged with grey, and his eyes were closed as he lay motionless on the stretcher. Duncan watched as the two EMTs rushed inside, trailed by three nurses in blue scrubs. His heart raced as he weighed his options—should he follow them into the hospital or take off? He knew if he stayed at the hospital, the creature might hurt more people trying to get to him. But he was desperately hungry and in need of more clothes. If they had made it sixty miles away, that would be far enough apart for a while, at least until dusk. Drawing a deep breath, he exited the ambulance and followed them inside.

Duncan nervously entered the emergency room and spotted an elderly duty nurse with a deeply wrinkled face and long, stringy gray hair standing at the entrance to the patient areas. He knew she wouldn't let him in without a proper explanation, yet he needed to get past her quickly to reach Gus. Taking a deep breath, he mustered up his courage and approached her. "Excuse me," he said softly. "They just brought my father in; I'd like to go in the back and be with him."

The nurse glanced down at the clipboard in her left hand, then looked back at Duncan. "What's your last name?"

He hesitated as fear seized his heart. He didn't want to lie outright but had no choice if he wanted to go to his friend's side. Summoning up a simple smile, he uttered one word: "Doug."

"No, your –" the nurse began before the ambulance driver peeked out from the doorway and called for Duncan. "Come on in," he said. "I was wondering what happened to you – I think you should get yourself looked at for heat exhaustion."

The nurse eyed the paramedic suspiciously over her wire-rimmed glasses resting halfway down the bridge of her nose. After deliberation, she sighed and allowed Duncan through the doors. He rushed past her with a wave of thanks and apprehension.

Duncan followed the paramedic down a dingy hallway, each step echoing off the surrounding walls. He heard muffled voices and beeping machines as they weaved around a corner and stopped at a light curtain.

"I want you to wait here," the paramedic said, pointing to one of the rooms. "The intern Doctors will work on Gus until Doctor Williams gets here. They will bring him in here when they finish up with him."

Duncan looked around at the bare room filled with medical equipment and back at the paramedic in disbelief. The area looked smaller from the outside.

He walked over to the sink and greedily drank several cups of water until his throat was soothed. A few minutes later, the paramedic returned to the room with a food tray and sat it on a small table in the corner.

"Go slow on the water, kid. Here's your food," he said with an air of kindness. "I probably won't see you again, so take care. I hope your friend pulls through; he seemed stable."

Duncan thanked him for his help as he watched him disappear behind the curtain for a final time, leaving Duncan alone. Taking one last glance around his room, he pulled back the curtain and stepped into the hallway. It was quiet and still, but the antiseptic smell and stark white walls were unmistakable; he knew he was in some hospital. He stood still for a moment, listening intently as he heard the heavy door at the end of the hall clang shut.

Cautiously, he opened the nearest door and crept inside to find an empty room with only a few gowns scattered around. A sudden realization hit Duncan like a wave as he spotted that these gowns were of a different color than the one he'd been wearing - meaning that he had to have come from somewhere else. He didn't even take the time to look through any of the drawers or closets before hurrying out again.

The duty desk in the middle of the hallway, opposite all the patient rooms, was still eerily unmanned. Duncan took advantage of this lack of supervision by slipping past it towards another room nearby. As he gently pulled back its curtain, Duncan's heart almost stopped when he saw an enormous man lying in bed. Desperate to not be detected, Duncan resigned himself to defeat and quietly left without checking if any clothing was present.

Fortunately, he found the hallway still deserted as he made his way to the next room. He crept inside, eyes widening at seeing a teenage boy asleep in the bed. His heart raced as he tiptoed to a tall closet and softly opened the door. He scanned through hanging items until his fingers touched a shirt and pants that would fit him perfectly – although they were slightly too long and wide for his frame, he fixed them with a belt from the closet. Bundle tucked beneath one arm, he navigated back to the hall where nurses had suddenly appeared, bustling about with their duties. No one paid attention to Duncan as he hurried back to his room, hoping no questions would be asked. Once inside, he pulled shut the curtain before slipping into the stolen clothes. Guilt tugged at him – he wanted to do right by the sick child, so he folded the overalls and placed them neatly in the corner of the room. Knowing there were no extra shoes, he decided to keep Doug's boots.

Hanging from the plain wall in the corner was a small circle clock. Its hands glowed a soft yellow-green, telling Duncan it was 2:07 p.m. He hadn't seen an accurate watch in what felt like ages, and seeing this one gave him a sense of comfort. The afternoon's still young, he thought. There were several more hours until dark and plenty of time for a meal before then.

Duncan's stomach grumbled in agreement, reminding him that he had a plate of food waiting for him. The bland, monotonous food had little flavor, but he didn't care – his hunger was satisfied, and his throat was wet with cool refreshment. Swallowing smoothly, he leaned back in his chair and rubbed his full stomach. He quickly ate his meal and finished it off with another glass of water from the sink.

He felt so satisfied that he couldn't keep his eyes open any longer; they weighed down heavily despite propping them open with his fingertips. His fingers slowly relaxed into the armrest, and sleep overtook him.

Instantly, he found himself back at the same place as his earlier dream.

This time the room was much creepier because he remembered everything from it. He was sitting in the same small room with no windows and only one door that seemed far too familiar to him. It felt like he'd spent an eternity there, yet his memory offered no help.

The room was pitch black, the only light coming from the thin strip that shone beneath the door. He knew this place, a dream so often visited, and he yearned for what lay beyond it. But he had to stay put, rooted in fear of the unknown.

From outside came muffled voices and snippets of conversation made faint by the thick walls. "The final sequence of DNA has been inserted into the designated spot in the genome, sir." A high-pitched voice said. "The computer is assembling all the information from each nucleotide; we'll have the full picture soon." Replied a deep scratchy voice.

He struggled to comprehend their words, but his attention was soon drawn away from them as he remembered something else - he wasn't alone in his dream. His gaze scanned the darkness until they fell upon a pair of glowing red eyes closing in on him quickly. The creature was back and moving closer.

CHAPTER EIGHT

The monster lumbered through the forest, its fur tangled and damp from the morning dew. It was running out of time. As much as it pained it, the boy's recovery would have to wait. He had to survive.

As the sun rose, the monster felt a surge of panic. It was tired and weak, its breaths shallow as it stumbled through the underbrush. It knew it needed to find shelter soon, or it would be caught in the open when the sun rose. It knew it needed to find a hiding place but was too weak to move. The sunlight crept closer, its warmth spreading across the forest floor. The monster closed its eyes, ready to face its fate. However, it remembered the boy and knew it needed to keep moving. It couldn't stop yet. It stumbled on its feet, its legs still weak, but its mind clear. It followed the tree line into the forest, searching for a place to hide from the daylight.

The monster's panic grew. Its time was almost up. It saw something in the distance when it thought all was lost.

A small hole tucked away in the side of a hill. The monster stumbled towards the cave, its legs shaking as it struggled to keep moving. As it stepped into the cool darkness of the cave, it felt a sense of relief wash over it.

The monster collapsed onto the cave floor, breathing ragged, but its heart filled with a new sense of hope. It knew it couldn't stay in the cave forever and would have to keep moving if it wanted to find the boy. But for now, it was safe, and that was all that mattered.

As the monster lay there, its eyes closed, it felt sad. It had spent its entire life in captivity, hiding from humans when it could and fearing the daylight. It had never known a life free from fear and pain.

As it lay there, listening to the sound of the morning animals outside the cave, the monster felt a glimmer of hope. It knew that there was more to life than fear and pain, that there was a chance for a better future.

The creature was on the move. Night had come and signaled the boy had a full day head start on him.

Humans hunted and feared the monster. It knew that going back out was necessary to find the boy, but it was apprehensive of the look-alike men. Even though he had lived his entire life in the shadows, always hiding, always quiet, he knew they would kill him. He would kill them first, just like the night before.

The creature had found shelter just in time the previous night, but by the time the sun had risen and he was forced to hide, there was nothing to eat and no water.

As it stumbled from the cave, the monster heard running water. It picked up its pace towards the sound, its legs heavy and its vision blurry. Finally, it reached a small stream, its waters clear and calm. The monster collapsed beside the stream, its chest heaving as it struggled to catch its breath.

But then something strange happened. A fish was staring up at him from the water. It reached down, grabbed it, and started to eat. When finished, he drank at the water until he felt his body reinvigorated.

The creature was now ready to resume his hunt for the boy. Re-freshed, it bolted off into the darkness.

CHAPTER NINE

Duncan's eyes flew open, and he sat bolt-upright in the chair. His heart began to race as he imagined the monster pursuing him again, its black form moving swiftly toward him. The last vestiges of the nightmare dissipated from his mind, but the fear remained. He looked at the clock – 8:02 PM – and realized with a jolt that he had been sleeping for hours; it was now nightfall outside.

"Oh no!" Duncan gasped, wiping away droplets of sweat from his forehead. "What have I done?"

Cautiously, he pulled back the curtain and stepped out into the hallway. He jumped back in surprise when he saw a uniformed policeman talking with a hospital doctor. Had they noticed something amiss? He crept forward on all fours, crawling through the curtain, across the hall, and pressing his back against the front side of the nurse's station to listen in on their conversation. To his amazement, he realized that it was not just any cop but the Sheriff himself speaking with Doctor Williams, Chief Physician of the hospital.

"Yep, he is still in surgery," Doctor Williams said, with a heavy frown knitting his eyebrows. "He's going to be fine, but it will be a few hours before he can talk. What did you learn about the FBI fellows looking for that boy?"

Sheriff McCoo exhaled slowly and ran his finger along the brim of his hat. "They did check out, but I couldn't find anything on any cases or projects looking for a kid that goes around slaughtering people as we saw in the diner. The slaughter in the diner doesn't seem to fit. I am sure that there is more going on here. We need to figure out what it is."

Doctor Williams nodded thoughtfully, adjusting his glasses on the bridge of his nose. "Well, you have circulated his picture. When you find the boy, ask him."

Hiding behind the nurse's station, Duncan heard every word and felt an icy chill run down his spine. Whatever the police or the FBI thought, he couldn't tell them what happened... not yet. He wanted to jump up and tell them they were wrong, but if they took him to jail, he would be trapped until the monster got to him. He had to escape. It was the only way to stay alive.

Staying low to the ground and against walls, Duncan edged down the aisle towards the door. As he got further away from them, their voices became muffled by all the activity around him. He heard Sheriff McCoo ask if Riley was still there, and Doctor Williams confirmed yes - he was in surgery with Gus looking after him like he had requested. The Sheriff stopped at the nursing station and waited for the nurse to return. It only took a few minutes.

The nurse was an elderly woman with a crisp white lab coat and thick black glasses that rested on the end of her beak-like nose. She peered over the sheriff's shoulder, squinting at the picture in his hands.

"Have you seen this boy?" asked the Sheriff.

"Sure. He's in the room right there," she said, pointing down the hall toward Duncan's room. "He came in the ambulance with the man in surgery from the diner. He said he was his son."

The doctor and sheriff exchanged glances, realizing this was not true. "Maybe they picked him up on the way," she said, pursing her lips. "Even though it's against the rules, they have been known to do that occasionally. It wouldn't surprise me."

With urgency, they approached Duncan's room and pulled back the curtain. Recognizing that his only chance of escape lay beyond the lobby doors, Duncan bolted for freedom. The old nurse raised her arm and shouted, "There he goes! He's headed out to the lobby!"

Sheriff McCoo whipped his gun and yelled, "Stop, or I will shoot." When it was clear the kid would not stop, he holstered his weapon and ran after the kid.

Duncan flew through the doors and skidded to a stop, the soles of his shoes squeaking against the lobby's marble floor. He spotted a narrow flight of stairs leading up to another floor, and without a second thought, he sprinted toward it. His eyes darted frantically as he searched for an escape—if he went outside, they would catch him. Staying inside was his only chance.

Sheriff McCoo and Doc Williams stumbled into the lobby seconds later, their footsteps echoing off the walls as they surveyed the now-empty room. "This way!" Sheriff McCoo barked and ran out of the lobby door.

The boy took off in the opposite direction, his heart pounding. As he ran up the steps, Duncan noticed that this part of the hospital was much more open than downstairs. Large sets of rooms lined one side of the hallway, while clusters of desks and waiting areas filled with chairs dominated the other side. He had been here before, at least once in his life, just like he had been to Disneyland and watched Saturday Morning cartoons and tasted Rocky Road Ice Cream. The memories came flooding back, but unfortunately, so did reality—the monster was coming.

Duncan picked up speed as he ran down the hall, passing countless empty rooms. Everything was quiet except his breathing and feet slapping against the tiles. When he finally reached the end of the hallway, an emergency exit sign glowed red above a door.

The far side of the floor had a huge sliding glass window. He tugged, and it opened, letting in a gust of cool night air. Duncan peered at the pitch-black street below and spotted a delivery van parked several feet from the building. He pursed his lips and sighed, bracing himself for what would come. He took one final look around to ensure no one was watching before taking a running start and leaping toward the van's roof. The wind howled in Duncan's ears as he dropped through the air, his eyes on the van's rooftop. He landed with a thud in the center of the roof but lost his balance and tumbled forward. He reached out desperately, trying to find something to keep him from falling off the edge of the truck and ending up headfirst on the unforgiving pavement in the parking lot below. His hands latched onto something where the metal sides of the van met the roof - just enough of a grip to arrest his slide toward danger. After a few moments to regain his composure, Duncan released his grip and dropped lightly onto the asphalt road. Scanning his surroundings cautiously, he started in a fast jog heading south, unsure why he felt such an urgent need to get away from this place. Little did he know he was leading an unwelcome guest into another populated area.

CHAPTER TEN

It was a typical quiet evening in the small town of Goldpan, California. Carol sat on her front porch, sipping a glass of Rum and Coke, and enjoying the warm breeze. She was lost in thought, thinking about her late husband and the memories they had shared in their home. Things were tough, but she was making do. Peaceful nights on the porch helped.

But suddenly, her peaceful evening was interrupted by a sound coming from her backyard. It was a strange sound, a cross between a growl and a roar. She stood up and walked towards the backyard, her heart racing with fear. She stopped at the wooden gate and debated whether she should go out back or not. Whatever made the noise sounded hurt. As an animal lover, she had to help it, even if there was a chance it was a mangy coyote.

Settling her nerves with deep breaths, she listened for a few moments. With no additional noises, she unlatched and opened the gate. Carol froze, unable to move or even breathe. She stood at the fence entrance and watched a figure emerging from the shadows. It was a monster, half dog and half gorilla, standing on its hind legs and staring at her.

The creature didn't move towards her but didn't run away either. It simply stood there, its piercing eyes locked onto hers. Carol started to sweat, and her mouth went dry. She tried to force her legs to take her back but was frozen with fear and curiosity. She had never seen anything like this before.

Without a sound, the monster suddenly turned and ran. It leaped the fence in one jump and disappeared into the small patch of trees behind her house. Carol stood there momentarily, still in shock, before rushing inside to call the police.

When the Goldpan Sheriffs' office arrived, Carol still shook with fear. She led them to the backyard and pointed out where the monster stood. The two uniformed men scrutinized the area, eyes scanning the ground for evidence.

And then, they saw it. A large, human-like footprint was imprinted in the soft dirt. It was much larger than any footprint they had ever seen before.

The two deputies exchanged worried glances. They had no idea what creature could have left such a footprint. They questioned Carol, but she couldn't offer any more information. She reiterated what she had seen, that it was a monster unlike anything she had ever heard of.

The town was already abuzz with rumors and speculation about the creature. Rumor had it that it had killed a bunch of guys out at old Gus's place. Some said it was a mutated animal, the result of experiments gone wrong. Others believed it was a monster from a horror movie sent to terrorize the small town. No one knew for sure, but either way, Carol knew that was what she had seen.

The deputies worked tirelessly to find any clues about the creature. They searched the woods and questioned anyone who might have seen or heard something. But despite their efforts, they came up empty-handed.

As the deputies drove away from her house that night, she knew she had seen something extraordinary, and that would stay with her for the rest of her life.

The sun had long since set, casting a deep blue hue over the quiet suburban neighborhood. The only sounds were the occasional car passing by on the main road and the distant barks of a neighbor's dog. But there was something else that the residents couldn't quite put their finger on. A feeling of unease hung in the air like a thick fog that refused to dissipate.

In one of the blocks' houses, a young boy named Max played video games in his room. He had been engrossed in the game for hours, oblivious to the world outside. But as he paused to take a break, he noticed the eerie silence. It was too quiet and too still.

Max shrugged off the feeling of unease and went back to his game. But as he played, he began to feel like he was being watched. He shrugged it off again, but the feeling only intensified. He turned around, but no one was there.

Max's heart raced with the sound of a low growl outside his window. He slowly turned to look, but all he could see was the darkness outside. He got up from his bed and slowly went to the window, heart refusing to stop pounding in his chest.

Max froze in fear, unable to move or scream. As he peered out, he saw something moving in the shadows. It was large and hulking, with glowing eyes that seemed to stare right through him.

The creature let out another growl, louder this time. Max could feel his body shaking as he tried to back away from the window, but his legs wouldn't move. The creature stepped forward, its shadowy form looming in the darkness.

Suddenly, Max's door burst open, and his dad rushed in. He grabbed Max and pulled him away from the window, his eyes locked on the shadowy figure outside.

"What the hell is that?" Max's dad whispered, his voice filled with fear. "I saw it in the backyard from the living room."

Max could only shake his head, unable to find the words to describe what he had just seen. The creature outside let out another growl, sending shivers down their spines.

Max's dad picked up the phone and dialed 911, but there was no answer. The line was dead. They were on their own.

The creature outside continued to pace back and forth, waiting for its moment to strike. Max's dad knew they had to act fast. He grabbed a baseball bat from the closet and headed toward the door.

"Stay here, Max," he said, his voice firm. "I'll take care of this."

Max watched in horror as his dad headed out into the darkness, the baseball bat raised above his head. The creature let out another growl, and Max could see the fear in his dad's eyes. But he was determined to protect his son.

The creature lunged at Max's dad, but he was ready. He swung the bat with all his might, connecting with the creature's head. It let out a deafening screech and stumbled back, stunned.

Max's dad didn't waste any time. He swung the bat repeatedly, each blow connecting with bone-crushing force. Max stepped out onto the porch.

"Get back inside," the father yelled.

On seeing the boy, the creature didn't fight back. Instead, it turned, sure it had made a mistake, and ran into the darkness.

The police arrived soon after they called on a neighbor's phone, but couldn't explain what happened. There was no evidence of the creature, no trace of anything that would suggest it had ever existed.

But Max knew the truth. He had seen it with his own eyes. And as he lay in bed, that was all he could think of.

CHAPTER ELEVEN

The orderly pushed the gurney into the emergency room, the squeak of its wheels echoing in the stark hallway. Deputy Michael Riley followed close behind, taking his duty to protect the victim seriously. He wanted to prove himself worthy to become Sheriff one day, even if it meant taking on mundane tasks. He yanked back the curtain and stepped aside for the orderly, but as soon as he looked at what was inside, the man screamed and ran off, nurses scattering from his path.

Riley's heart stopped when he saw what was in the room: looming before him was a monstrous creature with bright red eyes that seemed to pierce right through him. Its body was covered with dark fur and had a long snout that ended in a mouth of very sharp teeth. In its enormous hands were a pair of overalls which it sniffed thoroughly before dropping them on the floor and turning towards the paralyzed deputy. It hadn't realized he was there.

Deputy Riley's eyes widened at the sight before him, and he backed away from the door. The monster's massive paw reached through the opening, and Riley scrambled backward until he was safely tucked under a desk. He watched in horror as the beast crept out of the room, its fur shaggy and matted with blood. The nurses had cleared out at the sound of the first growl. The creature stood on its hind legs and looked around the empty emergency room. It caught sight of Gus lying still on the gurney and began sniffing at his feet, following the scent trail up his body until it reached his face. The monster hovered silently over Gus's still form, almost remorseful.

The door to the emergency room swung open, and two paramedics raced in, pushing an empty gurney between them. The same two men had been at the diner earlier in the day. They saw the monstrous creature and knew this was what could have caused all those deaths earlier. They shoved the gurney towards the monster, hoping to distract it, while escaping into the lobby.

Before they could make it far, the creature turned its attention to them and chased the frantic men out of swinging doors. After only a few steps, an odd look of realization spread across its face. It sniffed around while listening to the activity of more humans. It stopped chasing and returned to the room with the overalls.

It lunged through the windowpanes so hard that shards shattered onto concrete floors like confetti from a celebratory parade. Then it disappeared into the darkness toward the tree line.

Sheriff McCoo heard the screams of terror and rushed into the lobby from the parking lot. He maneuvered through the hospital and slowly approached the room. He could not believe the size of the hole that must have been made by whatever had people screaming. He saw people scattered about, cowering in corners and pushing past him in their panic. At the end of the hall, a window was smashed outward, shards of glass glinting in the orange light of the hallway lamps.

"What happened?" Doctor Williams said, running up behind him.

"Not sure," Sheriff McCoo replied, scanning the room for answers. "I just got here myself."

Both men rushed into the emergency room and found Gus lying still on a stretcher in front of his room.

Sheriff McCoo yelled out, "Riley! Where are you?"

Riley emerged from under one of the desks at the far end of the room with a sheepish expression. "I'm okay," he said, brushing off his pants.

The Sheriff felt anger rising inside him. He had asked Riley to protect this citizen, only to find him to hide away instead. He kept his cool and asked what had caused such destruction.

Riley explained that he had seen an enormous creature— more significant than anything he'd seen before— smashing its way down the corridor before crashing through the window. However, he was too scared to move. He had hidden under the desk until it was all over.

Doctor Williams checked over Gus and confirmed that he wasn't hurt any further, while Sheriff McCoo reprimanded Riley for leaving someone exposed when he'd specifically been asked to protect them. Riley apologized but pointed out that at least Gus was safe now. The Sheriff sighed and nodded.

As Deputy Riley spoke, all eyes were drawn to the desk behind him. He pointed, his jaw clenched and swallowed hard, "It was huge. Bigger than anything I've ever seen before. It had these big teeth and claws.

Before the Sheriff could respond, his cell phone vibrated in his pocket. He retrieved it, looked at the screen, and answered. "Sheriff McCoo."

The deputy on the other end spent a few minutes describing the scene they had just visited. The description of what the witness saw and the footprints' size sounded exactly as Riley had described. He thanked the deputy and asked him to go back out when he had a chance and make a mold of the footprints. After a few more instructions, McCoo hung up and turned back to Riley.

"I may have misjudged you," the Sheriff said. "There was a sighting earlier just a few blocks away. Why do you think it was here, Riley?"

"It was just sitting in that corner, sniffing a pair of overalls on the floor. The orderly and I came in, but it got spooked and lunged at us, so we ran." Riley started to shake more with each word.

The Sheriff stepped closer, cradling the overalls as he inspected them closely. "Kids size," he mused before glancing up and handing them to Doc Williams. "I think whatever is tracking him made the killing, and the FBI men are chasing the wrong thing." He paused for emphasis and then pointed down at the overalls. "Check inside the left strap label."

Doc read the label on the discarded cans and looked up. "These belong to Gus's boy," he said with a shake of his head. "But I'm sure he wasn't around here tonight."

"No, but maybe Gus had given the boy these or something," suggested McCoo. "Gus appeared to be concerned for the kid rather than afraid of him. I don't know if the boy answers our mystery, but he might be the key to unlocking it."

Doc thought it over before asking, "What do you suggest we do?"

"We should start by finding that boy," declared the sheriff. "And preferably before those FBI fellows arrive on the scene."

Duncan arrived in Goldpan less than an hour later. He quickly surveyed the town as he jogged through its cobblestoned streets. It had three long thoroughfares lined wall-to-wall with buildings that intersected neatly, forming a grid-like layout. Despite its cute appearance, it was nowhere near what Duncan was looking for; he needed something bigger—something livelier and more exciting.

Suddenly remembering something from his past, he stopped short in his tracks with a gasp. He was sure he was from a big city! The memory flashed before him like a movie screen but then just as quickly faded away into nothingness, leaving him frustrated at the lack of information it brought. Crossing his fingers, he hoped it would return. He wanted to remember more about himself and where he belonged.

Picking his jogging pace again, Duncan continued down Main Street, heading southward with newfound energy. Around him, the cold night air cooled his skin as he ran.

As he passed the Sheriff's office, Duncan noticed a man wearing an official uniform with a badge glinting in the moonlight. The Deputy was leaning against the post outside the building, observing his surroundings. When the man's gaze fixed on him, Duncan lowered his head and quickened his pace.

"Hey, kid," the Deputy called out. Despite the authoritative voice, his tone was gentle, as if he was concerned for Duncan's safety. "Get out of the street. You're likely to get hurt running at night."

Duncan glanced up at the officer, noting that he had not been recognized. He couldn't tell if this man wanted to help or trap him like all the others. Without waiting for a response from Duncan, the Deputy urged again, "Do you hear me?"

The boy forced down a lump in his throat and replied with a timid nod. He kept his eyes on the ground and muttered a quiet apology before daring to pick up speed again closer to the side of the road.

It seemed too good to be true when Deputy Johnson didn't pursue him further, and Duncan felt a sense of relief wash over him as he continued his escape. However, no sooner had these thoughts subsided than he heard another loud command behind him.

"Stop!"

Without even looking back, Duncan broke into a sprint and fled into the night.

CHAPTER TWELVE

The creature's long snout twitched as it tested the air, searching for the boy's scent. A faint trail of his unique aroma led off in two directions - one toward the back of the hospital and one to the town beyond. Knowing how important it was to find him, the monster had no choice but to follow both leads.

It followed the scent to a delivery van parked behind the hospital. It crouched low, launched into the air with powerful thrusts from its hind legs, and landed gracefully on the truck. Following the smell trail up to an open window, it pondered whether a human boy could have ever reached such a height. But it had no choice; if it missed him now, an even greater distance could separate them, and something else may happen.

The creature jumped through the hospital window and found itself alone on the upper floor of the building, the same room it had left only a short while ago. The air hung heavy with silence, yet its acute senses could still pick up traces of the boy's presence. With careful steps, it proceeded cautiously down each hallway and peered inside each room, eventually realizing he wasn't there.

The creature crept down the staircase, following the boy's scent to the lobby. Its ears twitched as it heard humans screaming in panic, but he resisted the urge to run to the bottom of the stairs. It saw two men enter from the parking lot - a Doctor and a Sheriff. The monster couldn't understand their conversation but could tell from their body language that they were searching for the boy too. Gathering its courage, it climbed back up the stairs and through an open window. It followed the boy's scent toward town, eager to bring him home.

CHAPTER THIRTEEN

Agent Lee had to focus his eyesight to see as he stepped out of the diner into the darkness. The bright lights of the restaurant had left him momentarily blind. His team of agents stood around the open side door of their van, silently surveying the scene surrounding them. Every last trace of the boy or the creature following him from the facility had been removed with diligent care, and all that remained now was for them to set it on fire so nothing could be found in a future investigation. Agent Washington knew what needed to be done - they'd doused the foundation in gasoline and drawn a direct burn line to the gas tanks beneath the station. The burn would leave nothing but charred rubble in its wake.

"The place looks spotless," Agent Lee commented before being interrupted by Agent Jones.

"We have just received a report from our insider in town," he called from within the van, his voice slightly crackling over an old radio receiver. "He says that he is still in place - no sign any of this has jeopardized his position, but more importantly, it appears the creature and the boy were both at the hospital. They are gone now, but they were seen."

As soon as he finished speaking, a concerned silence descended upon those gathered outside the diner. The Sheriff and at least a dozen other witnesses had seen the boy and creature together. This would make covering up their presence nearly impossible.

"This could get really messy," Agent Washington said quietly.

"I agree," Agent Lee replied, his features creasing into a frown of concentration. "That is too visible for us to make it disappear. Tell our contact to do as much damage control as possible and stay close to the situation so we can be alerted to any additional sightings or oddities."

"Yes, sir." Agent Jones picked up the headset resting by his hand, secured it over his ears, then leaned back in his chair and began tapping away on the console.

"This has the potential to blow up on us, sir," Agent Washington said, hands plunged deep into his coat pockets as he leaned against the side of the van.

"I will report everything to the General and let him decide. There is only so much we can control. We didn't create these monsters but are responsible for what happens now."

"Yes sir," Agent Washington replied.

Agent Lee stepped out of the van and glanced around the area one last time before producing a cigarette lighter from his pocket. He examined a small wet spot on the ground before him, then clicked open his lighter, lit it, and dropped it onto the pile. The flame spread out from its center in two directions – one towards the diner and another towards the gas pumps.

The fire first arrived at the diner and, within minutes, engulfed it, and immense flames tore down its structure with an eerie orange glow that could be seen for miles.

The second line of flame eventually reached its destination, an old gas pump left abandoned in front of a convenience store and, with a deafening roar, exploded skyward nearly a hundred feet before cascading back to earth in a shower of smoke and debris. The flame burned so hot that all the metal began to melt in on itself.

CHAPTER FOURTEEN

Deputy Johnson sprinted down Main Street, the wanted boy in his sights just a few steps ahead. His radio squawked from his belt, and he snatched it up to answer Sheriff McCoo's urgent call. "We are just passing Dooley's Pub," Johnson gasped between breaths. He could hear the sheriff already hitting the accelerator and speeding into downtown.

The kid kept moving, ducking into alleys, weaving around corners, desperate for an escape. Johnson ran like lightning, but the gap between them widened with every second. The deputy reached for his gun in its holster and shouted a warning, "Stop right there! No use running; I know you can hear me!" But the kid didn't listen and kept going.

Sheriff McCoo took it all in as he raced towards them in his cruiser, his deputies fast behind him. He saw the boy running around Dooley's Pub, pushing himself harder now that he was so close to capture. Just then, two of Sheriff McCoo's other deputies came from opposite directions and blocked any possible escape route. The air was tense as everyone stood at a standstill, unsure what would happen next.

Duncan's heart raced as he heard the Deputy's voice. He entered a set of double doors to his right and glanced frantically around the large lobby of the Hunchback Hotel. He noticed mismatched furniture, a stained rug spread over the wooden floor, and a desk with a faded sign due to years without care. In desperation, his gaze flew towards two narrow hallways flanked by doors on either side. The end of each hall was blocked by a window with thick iron bars sealing off any hope of escape from that direction. His last resort lay before him - an old flight of stairs heading into the darkness above. Without another thought,

Duncan sprinted towards the stairs, taking them two at a time. He could hear the Sheriff call for him to stop and answer questions. However, he couldn't bear to turn around and risk getting caught.

Duncan raced up the hotel stairs. His heart pounded against his ribcage as he reached the second-floor landing and continued climbing to the third. He threw himself into the dimly lit hallway, searching for an unlocked room, but all were tightly closed. Arms shaking with fear, Duncan checked each door handle until he was forced to concede defeat. There was no escape from this floor.

The premonition of danger tingling in his spine since he left the hospital room only intensified now, as if the creature chasing him was drawing near. He cursed his luck - how could he have been so stupid as to hope that by running and climbing a bunch of stairs, the police would be too winded to follow?

A sudden noise behind him made Duncan's blood run cold. The Sheriff and Deputy appeared at the top of the stairwell, panting heavily and barely able to stand on their feet.

Through labored breaths, Deputy Johnson spoke, "End of the line, kid, make this easy on yourself and come along peacefully."

Sheriff McCoo's face creased with a fatherly frown, his body rigid with indignation. He straightened up and looked Duncan in the eye. "Would you just please shut up?" he said calmly to his deputy.

Deputy Johnson stepped forward, reaching for his gun at his waistband. Sheriff McCoo noticed this and quickly raised his hand to stop him. "Put that away right now," he commanded sternly. "You might hurt yourself or, worse, someone else."

Duncan looked from one lawman to the other, uncertain of what to expect next.

The Sheriff softened his tone. "We can protect you at the station," he said gently. "We have a lot of armed men. We can keep you safe. But it won't be easy. I saw what that thing did to those people in the diner. You should have seen how much it scared the people at the hospital."

The Deputy sighed and slowly returned the gun to its holster. His lips tightened into a thin line as he nodded at the Sheriff's orders. "You don't have much choice, kid," he said gravely.

Duncan slowly walked towards them, and when he felt they had let their guard down, he pushed past them in a frantic run. He split them with a football move he had no idea he knew. His heart thumped wildly as his feet pounded against the stairs. His boots felt like anvils, burdening him with every step. He bent low and grabbed the railing to propel himself forward. The Sheriff's voice reverberated down the staircase, forcing Duncan to quicken his pace.

The two officers reached out to grab him, but Duncan dodged them and kept running. His lungs burned as his feet flew faster and faster down the steps. He replayed a childhood memory in his mind, which gave him the extra energy he needed to escape—until a new obstacle barred his way. Two more cops came up from the lobby, trapping him between them and the Sheriff. All of his hard work had been for nothing.

Defeated, Duncan stopped running and plopped down on the steps with a heavy sigh. Although he tried to make the best of a bad situation, he couldn't help but worry about what would happen next. Sweat dripped from his forehead as he looked up at the officers encircling him. Duncan's back was ramrod straight as he sat still.

The Sheriff and three of his officers surrounded Duncan, their faces stern and unrelenting. There was a brief pause before one of the officers stepped forward and grabbed him roughly by the arms. The cold metal of the handcuffs clinked as they encircled his wrists. He could hear murmurs from the other guests in the rooms nearby, each asking why so many men were needed to apprehend such a small child. The Sheriff didn't answer any of their questions. He just pulled Duncan along unwaveringly until they arrived at their destination.

Several camera phones captured the arrest of the boy. The onlookers didn't move to help the boy, which everyone was thankful for. McCoo wondered how long before it ended up on social media claiming police brutality. They didn't have the whole story, and the uninformed posts would bring a lot of attention to him. He was going to stop and collect the phones, but decided that would be a problem for another day. He had to figure out the boy and whatever was after him first.

CHAPTER FIFTEEN

Duncan shuffled into the police station with his hands cuffed behind his back. The second floor was small but open, with desks and chairs haphazardly lined up along the walls. A single computer sat lonely on a desk in the corner of the room; most officers eyed it suspiciously.

Sheriff McCoo unlocked Duncan's cuffs and gestured to a chair at a table in the center. "Give me your right hand," he said sternly, holding out his palm.

Duncan obeyed, reluctantly placing his trembling hand in the sheriff. McCoo took each finger one by one, rolling them across an inkpad before pressing them firmly onto a piece of paper in a small square formation. When finished, he handed Duncan a tissue to wipe the ink off his fingers.

"I haven't done anything," Duncan mumbled.

"You're right. You haven't done anything. At least not that we know of. We've got a fancy new computer here. Let's feed your prints into it and see what we can learn about you. I'm sure the feds wouldn't be bothered if there wasn't something to find, huh? Unless you want to tell me why they're after you?"

The Sheriff fed the paper with the fingerprints into a scanner and clicked on a few buttons on the screen as Duncan nervously fiddled with his sleeves. The small image of a rotating hourglass filled the monitor, indicating the system was processing information from law enforcement databases.

"Okay, let me clarify for you. I can't remember anything about me. I get hints occasionally, but nothing substantial or concrete. It's like waking up in an unfamiliar place without any recollection of how I ended up here or who I am," Duncan said, his voice trembling and face contorted with fear. He went silent for several agonizing seconds. He swallowed deeply. "Oh, my god. It will come for me. Nothing could have stopped it from getting Gus, Bill, and everyone else... Please, you have to let me go somewhere far away from people. I can feel it nearby now."

"I can't do that yet. Until you decide to be more cooperative and open up with some basic information, I'm going to assume that there's something you're deliberately hiding from us," the Sheriff said sternly as he eyed Duncan skeptically.

"Helpful? How can I help when I don't know who I am or what happened to me?"

Sheriff McCoo motioned for his Deputy to come over and join them at the table. Johnson, weary from the pursuit of the boy, reluctantly complied and shot Duncan a disapproving scowl. The Sheriff pointed to the computer's hourglass, which had started to move slowly across the screen. "When this stops moving, it will say completed. When you see that happen, just come, and get me. Got it?"

The Sheriff pulled Duncan towards him by his forearm and directed him down the corridor to a thick metal door with a small open window blocked by bars. Duncan dug his heels in, resisting and pleading for release, but the Sheriff only tightened his grip and pushed him forward.

As McCoo opened the latch and swung open the prison-like door, Deputy Johnson yelled from across the room, "Sheriff! The results have come out already. It says it's two pages worth!"

Sheriff McCoo gestured for Duncan to follow him back to the room and pulled up two pages of information about him with a few clicks from the computer keyboard. He forced Duncan into a seat and retrieved the papers. He read through them twice and, for good measure, did a third pass. Mumbling under his breath, he regained his glasses from his pocket and put them on.

Duncan watched anxiously, leaning forward on the edge of his seat, desperate to hear the answer to the only question that mattered, what was his name?

The Sheriff read down each line, mumbling softly under his breath. As he finished reading, he looked at Duncan and said, "Your name is Alex Carter."

Duncan sat back in his chair, confusion becoming comprehension as the pieces of his identity slowly became more apparent. A small smile spread across his face, but it quickly melted away as he thought of all the trouble he was in. But at least now he knew who he was.

The name felt right. That was his name. Before he could celebrate, Alex's mind whirled with memories and thoughts so overwhelming that he had to grip the side of the desk and squeeze his eyes shut to make it stop. He saw his family, friends, and a mountain trail where he had been riding a horse just moments before.

Sheriff McCoo cleared his throat, breaking into Alex's trance. He flipped through the documents and peered at Alex over his glasses. "It says here you are sixteen years old, with no record of any criminal activity."

Alex found himself relaxing until the sheriff continued. "According to this report, you died six months ago in a horseback riding accident."

The floor seemed to move beneath Alex's feet as an earthquake had struck. His vision blurred. The room spun around him like a merry-go-round gone mad. Alex reached for the edge of the desk but instead crumpled to the ground in an unconscious heap.

Sheriff McCoo handed the papers to his Deputy, who held them in a shivering grip, scanning the words as if they were written in a foreign tongue. He rushed around to the boy's side and shook him gently. When it became clear, Alex wasn't waking up. He shouted for someone to grab the first aid kit and its smelling salts.

CHAPTER SIXTEEN

Alex, formerly Duncan, he reminded himself, opened his eyes slowly, blinking away the foggy memories of his past. Hovering above him was Sheriff McCoo, his tall figure casting a long shadow along the stone floor. He seemed to be honest, but Alex couldn't help but feel a twinge of distrust when looking into his kind eyes.

"Sheriff, he's awake," the eager Deputy called from between the cell bars. The Sheriff leaned in closer to Alex.

"You gave us quite a scare there, Alex. Are you okay?" His voice was soft, almost soothing but did nothing to soothe the racing of Alex's heart.

"I think so," he replied, starting to sit up. "The last thing I remember is you telling me that I..." He trailed off, realizing he didn't know how to finish that sentence. What had happened?

"You fainted," Sheriff McCoo said gently, resting a hand on his shoulder. "Right after you heard that you had died in an accident."

Alex recoiled at the suggestion. "How can I have died? I'm walking around fine." His mind raced with questions about what could've happened before everything went blank for him.

"You said before you didn't remember who you were or what was going on with the Feds, and I almost believed you," the Sheriff continued, "but when I mentioned your name, Alex, you seemed to recognize it."

At the mention of his name, Alex's memories came rushing back until they stopped at the image of him being thrown from a horse. Everything after that was still gone. He shook his head slowly in confusion before responding.

"You want to call anyone?" the Sheriff asked, handing him his phone. "I have your mother's number in the file if you need it."

Alex slowly reached for the phone, his hands shaking with anticipation. He watched Sheriff McCoo give a slight nod of approval, dial the number, and placed the cell phone on speakerphone. Alex's heart thudded against his chest as the ringing echoed. On the second ring, a soft feminine voice came through the speakers. Tears welled in Alex's eyes as he recognized it was his mother, and her voice quivered as he spoke, "Momma, is that you?"

There was an ominous pause before his mother replied, her voice sharp and uncertain, "Who is this?"

Alex's voice trembled as he answered, "It's me, momma, Alex. Your son."

His mother quickly responded and shouted, "That's impossible! You are sick for doing this!"

Knowing he had no choice but to keep going, Alex explained, "Why, momma? Don't you recognize my voice? It's me, Alex. I'm up North somewhere."

Alex's hands shook as he held them clasped tightly on his lap. His voice, thick with emotion, cracked when his mom answered. Sheriff McCoo could tell that Alex was struggling to hold back tears. He could feel the dread in the room, heavy like a cloud, as Alex tried to explain who he was. But his mom didn't believe him.

"Mamn," the Sheriff spoke up. "This is Sheriff McCoo of the Goldpan Sheriffs' Department. This is real, and I assure you this is no joke. I am standing here with a young man who has the prints to confirm his identity."

Alex's mom was shouting. "You are sick, too. Trying to pull a cruel prank during my grief." She disconnected the call.

The Sheriff felt a sense of defeat radiating off the boy beside him. He took the phone away from Alex and re-dialed the number, but there was no answer. He dropped the phone back into his pocket and motioned for one of his officers to help Alex to a cell until they could figure out what to do next.

Deputy Johnson grabbed Alex by the arm and pulled him out of the chair, yanking him across the room without regard for the furniture he bumped into. Alex shuffled forward in silence, not bothering to fight or lift his head. As they passed through two doors, around a corner, and finally into a room with six barred cells, Deputy Johnson unlocked one of them and pushed Alex inside. The stench of rust and mold hit Alex like a wall as he stumbled towards the old mattress on a squeaky cot, collapsing onto it.

"For what it's worth. I'm sorry about that thing with your mother," Deputy Johnson said before walking off and closing the cell door behind him with a loud clang. In the sudden quiet, Alex was reminded of how alone he truly was.

Sheriff McCoo hung up the telephone and slowly rose to his feet. He had been trying to reach the boy's mother all morning, but she hadn't picked up. With a heavy sigh, he called the Federal Agents he had recently met and asked for their help. The agents agreed to come in a few hours, and he wasn't sure if it was the best move, but he didn't have many other options.

Suddenly, Deputy Johnson called from across the room. "Sheriff, Doc is on the phone up at the hospital."

The Sheriff reached for the receiver next to him. "What's up, Doc?" he asked with a hint of amusement in his voice.

"That will never be funny, John."

"We will have to agree to disagree. What do you need?"

"Gus has woken up," the doctor replied without further acknowledging Sheriff McCoo's lighthearted comment. "He should be able to talk to you if you want to come over."

"Has he said anything yet?"

"No."

"I'm coming over now." The Sheriff rushed towards the door. Halfway there, he remembered that the Federal Agents were on their way and stopped abruptly. "Johnson! I am going over to the hospital, but make those agent fellas wait for me before they talk to the boy - no matter what they say or do!"

"Yes, sir."

The Sheriff's office was small, with flickering fluorescent lights that cast a sickly pallor on everything. The Deputy slouched in his chair, lazily swinging his feet onto the desk as he listened to the men climbing the stairs to their station. He waited for them to give him an excuse to yell at them.

Knock! Knock! Knock!

Three FBI Agents stepped through the door, and the Deputy's hand hovered over his holster. They were like clones in their matching blue suits and sharp haircuts.

"What brings you, boys, out so late?" The Deputy said, trying to sound harsh but failing miserably. His voice cracked slightly as he spoke.

"It's only 8:00 pm," Agent Jones replied, straightening his suit. "Sheriff McCoo called us earlier today about your prisoner. We are here for the boy, Deputy."

The Deputy stiffened at the mention of the boy. He didn't want any trouble with the FBI. But he also didn't want to give up control.

"I'm afraid we cannot release him until the Sheriff returns," The Deputy said firmly, sweat beading on his forehead.

The Agents looked at each other and then back to The Deputy.

"We don't think you understand," Agent Washington stepped forward menacingly. "We are taking the boy."

Suddenly a dull thud echoed on the stairs outside the room.

"Is that a friend of yours out there?" the Deputy asked, grateful for any distraction from this situation.

Agent Jones said, "It's just us,"

Deputy Johnson slowly opened the door. He froze in disbelief at what he saw: a colossal beast peering in from the hall, its eyes glowing with anger and its claws extended. Its sharp fangs gleamed under a sliver of moonlight while it let out a growl. In a split second, the creature bounded into the room as Deputy Johnson stumbled backward in terror, reaching for the gun hanging on his hip.

CHAPTER SEVENTEEN

Deputy Rachel Jameson sped down the deserted highway, her patrol car's siren blaring through the night. The call had come in minutes ago—a gas station diner engulfed in flames, a scene of unimaginable horror: multiple murders, evidence gone up in smoke. The ominous glow in the distance grew stronger, casting an eerie red hue against the darkened sky. Rachel's heart pounded in her chest; anticipation mixed with trepidation.

As Rachel pulled up to the burning diner, the scene was chaos. Flames danced fiercely, devouring the building's structure, spewing black smoke into the atmosphere. The heat radiated through the windows of her vehicle, pressing against her face. Abandoned vehicles cluttered the parking lot, the remains of those who had witnessed and become victimized by the unimaginable. She hadn't been at the diner earlier when the bodies were discovered. However, she could imagine the carnage. If it weren't for the crime scene not being fully processed, she would have been happy to see the place burn along with the memories of what happened.

A shiver raced down Rachel's spine as she climbed out of her car, the sirens fading into the distance. Her boots crunched on the broken glass and debris that littered the ground. The acrid smell of burning wood and gasoline filled the air, making her gag.

The neon sign on the corner flickered, the once-bright letters now obscured by ash and soot. She stepped closer, taking in the charred remains. The remnants of the fire-ravaged interior were scattered across the ground. The horror of what had transpired here was etched into the smoky air.

Rachel's eyes scanned the surroundings, searching for any sign of life. The silence was haunting, broken only by the crackling of flames and the distant hum of approaching fire trucks. Panic clawed at her chest. If anyone had been in there and survived, they were likely long gone, fleeing from the monstrous inferno that had consumed this place. There shouldn't have been anyone, but you never knew.

Rachel moved cautiously toward the diner's entrance as the firemen arrived and battled the flames. The door's remnants barely clung to the hinges, a haunting reminder of the terror that had unfolded within. She peered inside, her flashlight cutting through the dense smoke.

The scene before her sent a chill down Rachel's spine. The diner's interior was a twisted, blackened maze of broken furniture and burned-out equipment. The booths and tables were charred skeletons, their once-vibrant colors reduced to ashen remnants. The walls were scorched, revealing glimpses of the exposed structure beneath.

Rachel swallowed hard, trying to push aside her fear and focus on her duty. The fire had consumed everything, leaving no trace of the evidence she had hoped to find. The arsonists had orchestrated their dark symphony, covering their tracks in a fiery symphony of destruction. But Rachel refused to give up.

She scanned across the wreckage, her eyes scanning for remnants that might hold a clue. But the flames had been ruthless, swallowing everything in their path. The once-promising crime scene now felt like a graveyard; the charred remains bearing witness to the unknown horrors that had unfolded here. She was just about to step back from the door and return to her car, but a flicker of metal caught her eye. She stepped across the threshold, careful not to go near the part of the diner still burning. In the corner sat two gas cans. She stepped back outside and went to her patrol car.

As Rachel moved further away, a flicker of movement caught her attention. She halted, her heart pounding in her ears. A figure emerged from the shadows, staggering toward her. It was a woman, her clothes tattered and her face smeared with soot. Her eyes held a haunted look as if she had witnessed something beyond comprehension. She opened her mouth to speak, but only a hoarse whisper escaped her lips. Rachel rushed to her side, supporting her trembling form.

"Did you see who did this? Can you tell me anything?" Rachel asked urgently, her voice laced with concern.

"I stopped for gas, and no one was here," she said. "I knocked on the door, but no one was there. I went to use the bathroom." She pointed to a group of portable toilets a hundred feet away.

"Did you see who did this?"

"I came out, and the place was on fire. They were driving away."

"Who did this?" Rachel was trying to stay patient, but it was hard.

The lady's gaze darted around as if she feared the perpetrators were still lurking in the darkness. "They... they were men in suits that looked identical."

Rachel had heard enough of the scene to know exactly who the lady was describing.

CHAPTER EIGHTEEN

The game ended in a stalemate. Alex sat quietly in his cell, staring at the thick layer of dust that coated the floor. He reached down, scrawled a tic-tac-toe design on the grimy surface, and filled the blank boxes with Xs and Os. He was never going to beat himself. He was just that bored.

Suddenly, a sharp scream pierced the air from the room across the hall. Alex's eyes widened as he recognized the sound he had heard when the creature attacked them in the diner. His stomach sank as he realized whoever else was in the other room was paying for his mistake.

"Let me out of here!" Alex shouted, shaking the iron bars that separated him from freedom. "I have to get away!" But no one answered his pleas, only gunshots and screams answered him from beyond the walls.

The sounds diminished until nothing, but silence remained. Alex listened intently at the cell door, straining to hear any sign of life from across the hallway. Suddenly, a loud crash erupted and echoed throughout the building - it was unmistakably that of someone breaking through the heavy hall doors.

"Who's there?" Alex asked. He squinted to make out the figure lurking around the corner of his cell. His heart raced, and his fingers trembled as he heard the guttural growl of the creature hunting him since he woke up. He pressed himself against the back wall, trying to melt into the darkness, and fixed his gaze on the entrance, steeling himself against whatever fate lay ahead.

The monster stepped into view - an enormous ape-like being with a canine head attached. Its long snout dripped saliva onto its chest, and each jagged tooth was stained red. With two giant hands, it grappled at the door bars, which creaked and screeched under pressure. The beast yanked hard, sending metal flying across the room, before dropping onto all fours and lumbering inside.

Alex felt a wave of terror wash over him. "Please don't hurt me," he begged, his voice shaking. "Whatever I did to make you mad, I'm sorry."

The creature advanced towards him slowly, taking one deliberate step at a time. It paused, cocking its head to the left with a combination of confusion and disbelief. Its eyes drooped as though it were trying to make sense of the situation, its snarling jaws shut.

Alex saw his chance. "I don't want to die," he pleaded hopefully.

The creature shook its head back and forth before slowly advancing towards him, stopping when only two feet separated them. It motioned to the dirt and began etching out something with one of its massive claws, each digit thicker than Alex's entire arm.

Once it had stepped aside, Alex could see the word DOGKEY etched into the ground for him to read. The creature nodded in recognition at the name and pointed towards its chest again.

Alex smiled nervously, not wanting to disrupt the peace between them. "Do we know each other?" he asked cautiously.

Dogkey grunted and began writing again in the dirt. Alex could make out most of it this time—the first three letters were clear, but the fourth was still a mystery. He tried to read it as best he could but couldn't decipher it completely.

"I don't understand that letter," he stated firmly before pointing to the ground again in question. "What did you mean there?"

Dogkey took his claw and more carefully drew each letter one at a time F - R - I – E – N – D – S. He scooted back from his work and pointed to it once more with absolute confidence.

Alex looked up from the dirt with an awe-filled smile as understanding dawned on him. "You and I are friends?" he exclaimed joyfully.

Alex looked up at the creature in disbelief. It stood tall, fur matted and stained with dirt and oil, an intimidating figure that he had only ever seen in his nightmares. Its eyes were wide and almost kind as they met his gaze.

"I don't remember anything. I'm sorry, but I can't remember you. My memory is completely gone," Alex said, gesturing to his head. "How long have we known each other?"

The creature bent over, its massive form casting a shadow over the ground. Its large paw scraped through the sand, leaving behind faint traces of letters.

Alex leaned closer, squinting to make out the words: "Six months." He sat back, confusion spread across his face.

The creature nodded and started writing again. Alex read each letter. S-A-V-E-Y-O-U.

"Save me? Do you know if I was in an accident or something? Were we in some hospital together?" he asked, remembering waking up in a strange hospital gown.

Dogkey bent down again, tracing another sentence before returning from the makeshift canvas. Alex felt a chill run up his spine when he read: "We were tests. The last test lost memory. We live in a metal tomb." Looking up at Dogkey disbelievingly, he noticed that its looming figure seemed more sorrowful than menacing. "Is that what you are? A test? I mean, what we are?" he asked gently.

The creature shook its head no and began to write again on the dust-covered ground, pausing every few seconds to survey the sentences before continuing. Alex read the new phrase: "I am Dogkey, and we friend. The test is what they do, not what we are." His eyes met Dogkey's, and a smile spread across his face as he understood the creature's words, feeling comforted by their newfound understanding. Dogkey's furry arms wrapped around him briefly, squeezing him lightly before backing away with a wide grin plastered across its canine-like face. The creature bent over one last time and furiously scratched something into the dirt-covered ground with tremendous force. "I missed you," Alex read aloud as he glanced down at what the creature had written.

Alex slowly raised his gaze and locked eyes with Dogkey, the silence between them almost tangible. He could see a million questions in the canine's brown eyes as he hesitated before finally mustering the strength to form his query. His voice cracked when he asked why Dogkey had killed all those people if he was looking for him.

The large dog cocked its head while considering his words before scratching into the dirt with a thick paw. Alex leaned closer, listening intently as Dogkey started writing complex sentences while speaking each word aloud. "Didn't kill them. Was protecting Alex. Men hurt Alex; all men bad." He shook his head wildly, desperate to explain that not everyone was terrible; the people at the diner hadn't done anything wrong. But it seemed his pleas were falling on deaf ears. The scratching steadily increased in intensity as Dogkey wrote with more determined strokes: "Dogkey did not kill them. Dogkey protects Alex. Alex's friend. Dogkey not let men hurt him."

It took a few moments for what the animal was saying to click in Alex's mind as understanding dawned on him; it was his fault those men had died; Dogkey thought they would hurt him and was trying to protect his friend from danger. An icy chill slithered down his spine and sank deep into his chest as guilt overwhelmed him. What would he do now?

CHAPTER NINETEEN

Alex slumped onto the cot, its frame groaning under his slender frame. An overwhelming sadness suddenly overcame him; every heavy breath he took reminded him of the men he had unwittingly caused to be hurt. His mind raced as he desperately tried to make sense of the situation, searching for a way out. He felt guilty but determined to prove that Dogkey no longer had to hurt people.

Dogkey laid his head down and pressed his muzzle against Alex's arm, tenderly licking his hand with a long, wet tongue. Alex looked into Dogkey's eyes and saw something he hadn't expected: an unmistakable glimmer of compassion.

He reached out and ran his hand across Dogkey's fur as he spoke tenderly, trying to explain what such behavior could mean for both of them: "You don't want to hurt anyone else now, do you? No killing - that's wrong - we understand that, right? We can go somewhere away from people so nobody gets hurt. Okay?"

Dogkey's eyes drooped, radiating guilt and worry in a way that reminded Alex of his dog when he had been caught sniffing around the kitchen. He reached out to pat the creature's head. "I know you didn't mean to hurt anyone, but we must be careful now. I won't leave you alone," he said softly.

Dogkey nodded before scrawling something in the dirt with a small claw. Alex squinted at it in the dim light and read, "Close your eyes."

He furrowed his brows in confusion but obeyed Dogkey's request and shut them tight. Dogkey waved one paw in front of Alex's face a few times to ensure he wasn't peeking, then carefully scooped him up onto his back. Even though he had been terrified of Dogkey just moments before, Alex relaxed into him, feeling comforted by the creature's warmth against his skin. With one swift movement, they were off into the night.

Alex felt a hand on his shoulder and heard footsteps in the hallway as Dogkey steered him out of the cell. The smell of stale, coppery blood hung heavy in the air as they reached the main hall, and Alex knew there was destruction around him; he clenched his fists and willed himself to keep his eyes shut.

The creature guided them down a winding staircase into the night air, where a fresh breeze rustled through Alex's newly stubbled hair. He opened his eyes, expecting to see the sidewalk in front of the police station littered with carnage, but instead saw only empty streets stretching before them; Dogkey had been too embarrassed to show Alex what he had done. The creature turned his head towards Alex and looked expectantly, wondering where they would go next.

"Let's go south," Alex said, pointing over Dogkey's shoulder toward the left. "I think it's that way. We need to go to my mother. I have to find out why everyone thinks I am dead."

Dogkey shot him a confused look before turning back to the road ahead. Alex smiled slightly; this was good progress. Maybe today, he'd finally get some answers.

Dogkey nodded and headed south, their footsteps echoing in the still night air. No one was on the street, and the two friends exited the town without problems. They left the road behind and ventured off into the desert, following a faint trail in front of them. The sands shifted beneath their feet as they walked, each step bringing them closer to their destination.

CHAPTER TWENTY

Sheriff McCoo finished talking to Gus and thanked him for his time. As he exited the room with Doc, he shook his head in disbelief. "If you ask me, I think he has lost it. The things he said he saw...he sounds crazy."

"He's been through a lot," Doc replied. "Is he on some drug that would make him see things or think he saw something he didn't?"

"Not at all, I gave him something for the pain, but that's it. There was only a little alcohol in his system, but not enough to cause hallucinations. What he said he saw, he thinks, is real. And it goes along with what the witnesses say they saw earlier tonight."

"There is no such thing as a half-dog, half-monkey creature."

"I wouldn't be surprised in this world," Doc said. "You never know. In college, we went through the science of gene manipulation. It was fascinating."

McCoo sighed and glanced out the window before turning back to Doc. "Okay, Mr. Scientist-- if it exists, how did it get here? Where did it come from?"

Doc smiled slightly and shrugged his shoulders. "I fix people—you solve the mysteries."

McCoo frowned, scratching his chin thoughtfully. "And I still can't see how this boy fits in it all-- Heck, he doesn't seem to know either. Says he has amnesia or something."

Doc's brow furrowed in surprise. "Amnesia? He said that?"

"Well, not exactly," McCoo answered. "He said he couldn't remember when I told him his real name. He started remembering some stuff.

But still claims he doesn't know what's going on or why that thing and the Feds want him so badly."

The doctor looked at Sheriff McCoo through horn-rimmed glasses and said, "It could be that he hit his head or was scared by something, or perhaps a combination of both. He most likely has temporary amnesia, usually brought on by some trauma. It should clear up in time. However, I can give him a once-over to verify. Does he at least remember people he has met or other recent memories?"

"Not sure, but I would guess yes."

"It can vary. I will let you know when I am able to check on him."

Sheriff McCoo smiled, thanked the doctor, and headed towards the door. He stopped and turned around, "You look like you could use some rest, too, Doc."

The doctor smiled sleepily and nodded. "Take care of yourself, Sheriff, and I'll let me know if Gus's condition changes."

"I haven't eaten all day, and I'm sure it's going to be an all-nighter. Want to go get some food and coffee?" McCoo started towards the door and stopped.

The doctor looked back at Gus and then the Sheriff. With a nod, he said, "Sure. But not at Gus's place."

"No shit, Sherlock."

"Keep digging, Watson."

"We will just go over to Martha's; I think she is open until 2 am." With a wave of his hand, Sheriff McCoo and Doc headed out.

CHAPTER TWENTY-ONE

Alex and Dogkey had been running for hours, his heart pounding in his chest. The creature had encouraged Alex to get on his back, but Alex was still unsure of trusting his new friend. When he saw the abandoned building, Alex didn't think twice before ducking inside, hoping that he could find a place for them to hide.

The abandoned building was eerie and silent, the only sound coming from the occasional creak of old wood or the rustle of debris as the wind blew through the broken windows. It was dark and dusty, the air thick with the smell of decay. He guessed it had been an old two-story mining warehouse back when there was still gold in the hills. Now empty, he was convinced there would be no one here.

Alex could barely see a few feet before him, and he knew that the monster lurked right behind him, waiting to pounce at the first sign of danger. Even though Dogkey would protect him, he was cautious to protect whatever he came across from him. He tried to stay quiet, his breaths shallow, as he crept deeper into the building.

Further into the building, Alex saw signs of life. There were old mattresses on the floor, discarded clothes piled up in the corners, and even an old stove used recently. He was surprised that other people lived in the abandoned building but didn't have time to wonder about it. Even though the squatter wasn't anywhere to be seen, he had to keep moving, keep searching for a place to hide. The sun would probably be up soon.

Finally, Alex found what he was looking for. A small room, tucked away in the corner of the building, with a door that locked from the inside. Alex breathed a sigh of relief as he closed the door behind them, knowing they were safe and could rest in peace.

Almost as soon as Alex had locked the door, he heard people outside. It was scratching on the floor. Alex's heart raced as he tried to figure out what to do. He prayed the door would hold and the homeless people would not attempt to break it down and discover the strength of Dogkey. But the relief was short-lived.

"Shhh," Alex whispered. "We must stay quiet so those people won't bother us."

Dogkey grunted and started towards the door. Alex stepped in front of him and put his hand on his chest. The two made eye contact, and Alex was frozen in terror. The monster snarled, barring its teeth, ready to pounce. But then something strange happened. It hesitated, sniffing the air as if it could smell the harmlessness of the people on the other side of the door. He blew a breath through his nose and backed away.

In desperation, Alex looked around the room, searching for anything to help him get comfortable. And that's when he saw it. A pile of old rags and sheets lying on the ground. It wasn't sanitary looking, but Alex was too tired to care.

The room was utterly dark, and the sun rose through a slit covering the window. Momentarily grateful for their safety, he lay down and closed his eyes. Dogkey moved next to him and sat down, keeping watch.

"You need to sleep, too," Alex said. "The door is locked."

Dogkey looked between him and the door a few times before deciding. He lay on the floor between Alex and the door, ensuring he could see the door from his spot.

The people in the main part of the building quieted down, and Alex guessed they had gone to sleep. With shaking hands, he picked up a pipe on the ground near him, holding it tightly as he stared at Dogkey. He held his breath, listening intently, but all he could hear was his heart pounding in his ears. It wasn't long after that before he drifted off to sleep.

CHAPTER
TWENTY-TWO

Sheriff McCoo sat in the small-town diner, his half-empty coffee cup in front of him. He looked tired, the dark circles under his eyes evidence of the long hours he had spent investigating the murders at the old diner and gas station on the outskirts of town.

"Say that again," said McCoo.

Across from him sat his best friend, Doc Williams. The doctor was a tall man with a lean build, his sharp features giving him an almost hawk-like appearance. He looked equally troubled as he repeated, "I think the thing after the boy is more scared of us than we are of him."

"I very much doubt that."

"I mean...sure...in a fight, it knows it's tougher. I think it tries to avoid us."

"How do you explain the diner?"

"Not sure. I know it doesn't fit my logic, but maybe we should focus on the boy, not the creature."

"On that, we are agreed. However, we still need to protect this town."

The Sheriff's cell phone began to ring. He retrieved it, looked at the screen, and answered it, "McCoo."

"Ohmygodsheriffitisaninvasion. Themonsters arecomingafterus." The deputy on the other end was talking very fast. McCoo couldn't understand and had to stop him to have him start again.

The deputy sighed, took a deep breath, and said, "We are getting reports of the mutant thing all over town. We have been dispatched to several locations; each description is the same. This thing is either moving all over town or an invasion."

"I'm sure if there were an invasion, we would know. Focus on the reports. Was anyone hurt?"

"That's the strange thing. One guy even hit it with a bat, and it still didn't tear him up. What do you make of that?"

Sheriff McCoo rubbed the bridge of his nose. "Not sure. About what time did these happen?"

"Different times, but after dark."

"That tracks. Thanks for the update. Let me know if anything else happens. I want to stay in the loop and keep up the good work out there."

"Yes, sir. Thank you."

"What's up?" Doc asked after McCoo returned his phone to his pocket.

"There are a few reports of the creature from residents. It is being seen all over town and freaking folks out."

"Do we need to go?"

"We can finish the meal. No one was hurt."

"That's weird."

"It is to me, too. Maybe you're right; we should focus on the boy."

"You should just listen to me always without question."

The Sheriff chuckled, sipped his coffee, and said, "Seriously, what do you make of it?"

Doc leaned forward; his eyes locked onto McCoo's. "Well, it's certainly not a typical animal attack," he said, his voice low and serious. "There are inconsistencies in the way the victims were killed. It's almost as if something or someone deliberately tried to make it look like an animal did it. If we hadn't had it visit us at the hospital, I would have claimed it a hoax."

McCoo raised an eyebrow. "You mean like a human in an outfit?"

Doc nodded. "It's possible. And if that's the case, we could be dealing with a serial killer. But it is hard to ignore the creature at the hospital.

Maybe both are true since the creature didn't kill anyone in town. It is real, and there is someone more human to blame."

"Interesting thought." McCoo leaned back in his chair, his mind racing. "We've got to catch this thing, Doc. Before it kills again."

"I couldn't agree more, but we have to be careful. We don't want to scare it off or make any mistakes. I go back to our focus on the boy."

McCoo nodded in agreement, his mind already thinking about the next steps. "I'll have the department look into the suspicious activity in the area. Maybe we can catch a break."

Doc reached out and put a hand on McCoo's arm. "Listen, I know this has been tough on you. But it would be best if you took care of yourself too. Don't let this case consume you."

The Sheriff sighed. "Easier said than done, Doc. I can't help but feel responsible for the safety of this town."

Doc shook his head. "You can't control everything, John. But you can do everything in your power to stop this killer. We'll catch it, I promise you."

McCoo nodded, a small smile appearing on his face. "Thanks, Doc. I needed to hear that."

"If nothing else, maybe it's bigfoot."

"Great. That's all we need in town. Bigfoot hunters are crazy."

They finished their food and were about to part ways when the Sheriff's phone rang again. "McCoo."

"It's me again, Sheriff." The deputy from earlier was on the phone again and seemed more shaken than before.

"What's up now?"

"The diner, sir."

"What about it?"

"Someone set it on fire, and it is going to burn to the ground."

"That's just great. Do we have anyone out there?"

"We have a car on the way. The Fire and EMT departments are already on the scene. I just wanted you to know since we did not finish processing the scene."

"Thank you. Keep me in the loop."

McCoo disconnected his phone call.

"I know that look on your face," Doc said. "What's happened now?"

"Someone set the diner on fire, and the Fire department can't save it. All that evidence is gone."

Doc's eyes widened. "How? Why?"

"Both are good questions. It could be that someone is trying to cover their tracks. I am going to drive out there. Want to come?"

"Nah. I should get back to the hospital."

"Want a lift?"

"It's okay. I can walk. Good luck out there."

"Thanks."

The Sheriff climbed into his car and sped off. He called ahead on the radio to let them know he was coming. He knew the diner fire was going to be a setback. However, he was more concerned about the treacherous road ahead to find this monster.

CHAPTER TWENTY-THREE

Sheriff McCoo turned the wheel of the patrol car, guiding it quietly down the road. He checked his rearview mirror, expecting to see the creature there, but all he saw was an empty stretch of asphalt illuminated by the full moon above. His mind raced over the grizzly details Gus had given him: a creature tearing through the multiple men like paper dolls, leaving behind nothing but destruction. And now, the diner was gone, and with it, all the evidence.

As he drove past the faded blue sign announcing the edge of town, Sheriff McCoo noticed something odd--the radio was silent. He had talked to his one deputy, but no one else was talking. This was common for his deputies at this time of night, but everyone was up and working, and he couldn't help that it didn't feel right. He picked up the mic and pressed the button. "Sheriff McCoo, to the station, come in." He waited a full 60 agonizing seconds. "Station report. I need to talk to you guys."

There was no answer for several moments before a sleepy voice crackled back. "This is Beller, sir. What do you need?"

"What's your location?" The Sheriff asked.

"Ungst and I are at the Aweds property," Beller replied. "A coyote attacked the Aweds' chickens, so we're taking statements, but it's awfully late...is everything all right?"

"The station isn't responding," Sheriff McCoo said gravely. "I want you to drop everything and meet me there—something is wrong."

The line went quiet momentarily before Beller said, "10-4, Sheriff." "It should take us about forty-five minutes to get there," he added quickly. In the background came the sound of an engine starting up and tires crunching against gravel as Beller and Ungst headed out.

"Drive fast," Sheriff McCoo commanded before putting down the mic. He turned the car around and headed back into town.

Sheriff McCoo's hands shook as he dropped the microphone back in its holder. The wind whipped through the open windows, casting an eerie foreboding over him. Reaching Main Street, he slammed on the brakes outside the stationhouse and jumped from his seat. His hand automatically reached for his holster. Heart pounding, he crept up to the doorframe. He shouted a warning before cautiously stepping inside, his gun drawn and at the ready.

Tiptoeing up the stairs, Sheriff McCoo paused to avoid creaking boards that could give away his position. Peering around the corner of the hallway, he looked into the squad room and observed a stillness in stark contrast to his racing pulse. He counted to ten, then thrust himself inside to find it empty - no one alive or breathing in sight.

The Sheriff was met with a horrific scene. Dead bodies were scattered around the room, some clawed and bitten by a creature that had exceeded any strength or brutality his men could have anticipated. The three federal Agents' clothing indicated them as the primary target of this monstrous attack - their bodies mangled to an almost unrecognizable state. He felt his stomach gurgle at the sight, but he kept its contents down.

Turning towards the confinement area, the Sheriff noticed the metal door to the cellblock had been ripped away from its frame. Racing through it, he quickly moved down the hall and into the boy's cell. It was empty - its metal barred door had been torn from its hinges and thrown aside- two giant handprints imprinted into where it must have been squeezed too tight to hold. There was no body, no blood. It seemed the creature had taken him with it rather than killing him. But why?

The Sheriff's eyes scanned the dusty floor of the cell until he spotted something odd - words written in the dust. He stepped inside, angled himself to get a better view, and deciphered what it said: "Close Eyes." His brow furrowed as he wondered what that could mean. Who wrote it, and why would they want the kid to close his eyes? Before he could continue pondering, a voice interrupted him from behind.

"They are working together," the voice said.

The Sheriff spun around, dropping to one knee with his gun aimed at the source of the sound. Agent Lee of the FBI stood there, calmly watching while the Sheriff got up and holstered his weapon.

"You shouldn't sneak up on people. I could have shot you," Sheriff McCoo said.

"I'll remember that," replied Agent Lee dryly.

"What do you mean they are working together? I talked to the kid; he was scared of that monster. No way they were doing this thing together." The Sheriff challenged.

"That's where you're wrong. They are friends- they have been for about six months. Why do you think there's no body for him? Many dead people are here, but you won't find the boy anywhere. Tell me I'm wrong?" Agent Lee asked sarcastically.

The Sheriff locked eyes with him briefly before replying steadily, "That's what I thought. They left together."

"I'm tired of your games. What is going on here? What aren't you telling me? I want to know." The Sheriff demanded.

Agent Lee's response was simply a flicker in his expression before he calmly and concisely refused to explain further. He glared at the Sheriff. He reached for the gun holstered to his hip and slowly pulled it from its leather casing, aiming the barrel directly at the Sheriff.

The Sheriff's eyes widened in surprise, and he opened his mouth to speak, but Agent Lee cut him off. "Unfortunately, you have decided to take this route," he said coldly. "I am afraid you won't be making any phone calls."

The Sheriff scoffed in disbelief. "What are you going to do, shoot me?" he asked, attempting to hide the tremor in his voice.

"If you don't do as I say, yes," Agent Lee replied without missing a beat. He looked over his shoulder and shouted, "Agent Michaels! Agent Brown!"

Two more agents with identical uniforms joined them, standing at either side of Agent Lee. He gave them a curt nod before turning back to the Sheriff.

"Report," he said sternly.

Agent Michaels approached Agent Lee, his senior. "Young says that the boy and the Monster were here less than an hour ago. We might be able to catch up to them pretty quick if we knew what direction."

Agent Lee smiled wickedly, making no attempt to hide his satisfaction. "Good news. Please lock the good Sheriff in one of his cells, then join me outside. I am sure the kid will head south. We should be able to project where they are headed and cut them off."

Sheriff McCoo's face was contorted with anger and frustration as he said, "You can't do this!"

The Federal Agent laughed condescendingly. "Oh, I certainly can and will. It never ceases to amaze me how idealistic and naïve some of your local law enforcement types are. I mean, really, what did you think you could do against a group of well-equipped Federal Agents? We have so much more power and resources at our disposal – enough to go to my head, I suppose."

Sheriff McCoo shot him a fierce look, growling through gritted teeth, "I will find a way to bring you down. I guarantee it."

Agent Lee snorted derisively before signaling to Agent Brown, who stepped forward and took the Sheriff's pistol from its holster without resistance. He then pushed him towards a cell with a firm hand on his shoulder. Sheriff McCoo wanted to fight back, but it would've been futile against two armed men; he had no choice but to yield or face certain death. With McCoo secured in a cell, Agent Lee turned and left the room while Agent Brown stayed behind to keep watch.

Sheriff McCoo's eyes widened as Agent Brown slammed the steel bar door behind him, reverberating through the narrow cellblock. He was surrounded by cold concrete and iron bars stretching to the ceiling, starkly contrasting his normally bustling station house. He could feel the desperation bubbling inside him as he grasped the horizontal bars of his cell door. "Listen to me," he pleaded, trying to keep the fear from his voice. "Lee may be rogue, but you two know this is wrong and should do something about it."

Agent Brown gave him a wry smile. "We are all rogue," he said. "You're a smart man. Figure it out."

The Agent left Sheriff McCoo alone in the cellblock, and he shook at the door with increasing ferocity. The rust on the hinges indicated that it had seen little use, leaving him trapped until his deputies arrived. The sounds from the other room told him the agent had laid down on their couch. He guessed he wouldn't be going anywhere soon.

CHAPTER
TWENTY-FOUR

Alex and Dogkey slept the day and a large portion of the night. The exhaustion claimed their lead. As soon as they realized, they took off traveling south. After what could only have been a few hours, the dark was disappearing.

Alex's heart raced as he looked up and saw the sun peeking over the horizon. He had to find shelter for himself and his new companion quickly or risk exposure to the sun's harsh rays. He pointed to an old, decrepit house in the distance, and off they ran.

Dogkey stopped at the house's entrance before gently lifting Alex from his back. With a quick brush of his hand, he cleared away the dirt and grime that clung to Alex's skin.

"Thank you," Alex said as he opened the door to the abandoned home.

The smell attacked their senses. It was a mixture of death and excrement. Alex's eyes started to water as he quickly covered his nose. Dogkey's enhanced senses had to be screaming. Although, it didn't show any sign of disgust.

The two explored every room until they found a small bedroom with one window shaded by thick curtains; it seemed this room would be their best bet at avoiding any sunlight sneaking through. The source of the smell was not apparent. However, some rooms were stronger than others. Something must have died in the walls.

They lay down on the hardwood floor, and tiredness instantly overcame them, allowing them to sleep soundly in their haven's darkness. Alex was thankful that the room was not the source of the smell, and it was hard even to notice when the door was shut.

Alex slowly opened his eyes to the familiar darkness of the tiny room. He was sitting in a faded red chair, surrounded by cold stone walls with no windows and only one door, from which a small stream of light crept through the gap at its base. A deep yearning for the light consumed him, but this time he was determined to keep it inside instead of giving in to fear as before.

He felt Dogkey still in the room and called out for him softly. "Dogkey, are you there?"

The monster stepped forward through the light so Alex could better look at him; the faint glow under the door now illuminated his soft, caring eyes. Alex hugged him tightly, whispering words of assurance that they would find a way out of their prison. But Dogkey shook his head sadly. He had resigned himself to an eternity in captivity, doomed to endless experiments and inevitable death in this cell.

Suddenly, the door burst open, and bright white light flooded the room. Dogkey cried out in pain, shielding his eyes with his paw-like hands and scurrying back into dark corners as he whimpered in agony.

"Take T-DNA Chromosome 19 experiment 29 to table thirteen," a deep-voiced man bellowed from outside the open door.

Two men in crisp white coats stormed into the room and grabbed Alex by each arm. Dogkey whimpered and ran for the shadows, but his movements were immediately halted when the light bulb above him exploded and rained shards of glass that sizzled and melted against his skin. He howled in agony and retreated further into the darkness.

Alex was dragged from the room, and Dogkey couldn't help. It had to protect the boy. Three times he burst into the light and felt the intense pain. It tried to move forward and fell to the ground. With a struggle, it dragged itself back to the shadow.

"Where are you taking me?" Alex shrieked as he fought against the grasp of the lab coats. His eyes widened when he discovered himself amidst a flurry of activity. A line of identical doors lined two walls, around twenty altogether. People scurried back and forth, donning starched lab coats with pockets full of pens and clipboards. No one spoke. They dragged him down the hall, through him into a room, and locked it behind him with a sickening click. What was this place?

"You are feeling feisty today. I see," the man with a deep voice said. There was a click, and one wall of the room became transparent.

Alex cowered back from the tall, imposing man. His shadow loomed over him through the glass, and his deep voice sent chills down Alex's spine. The man had short white hair cut close to the sides, a square jaw that seemed to be carved out of stone, and a large, jagged scar stretching from one side of his cheek to the other. Something about the healed wound felt familiar, like it belonged to someone he once knew: Dogkey.

The two white-coated men stepped back through the door and grabbed hold of Alex's arms. He tugged against them but found their grip to be ironclad. Alex tried to break free but couldn't budge an inch, no matter how hard he pulled. They quickly lifted him onto a cold metal table in the center of the room and secured his wrists and ankles with thick straps.

A petite female assistant with silver-rimmed glasses came beside him and pressed various points on his neck and chest. When she tilted his head to the side at a forty-five-degree angle, her eyes scanned the back of his neck before taking notes on her clipboard. Around him, additional masked figures remained silent as they wrote frantically on their clipboards.

Alex's heart raced as the scarred general loomed over him with a smirk, signaling accomplishment. His mind swirled with questions: What had this man done? Was he changed or combined with something like Dogkey? He wanted to ask but knew he wouldn't get the answers.

Reluctantly, he let the process unfold and waited to see what would happen next.

The assistant poked and prodded at Alex, placing instruments on his skin before reporting to the General. "It has healed one hundred percent," he said. "There is scarring where the neck broke, but no trauma to the muscle or bone beneath the layer of skin. It appears the procedure was successful."

Alex furrowed his brow in confusion; what procedure were they talking about? But before he could inquire further, the General spoke again. "Wonderful. I knew that transfecting the cell with lizard RNA to control the production of reptilian enzymes would act as a catalyst for the growth of the ends of chromosome 19 by more than 100 base pairs," he said with a satisfied smile. "Take his stats. I want to know his temperature, blood pressure, and white blood cell count. In addition, please check his pulse rate before and after we have completed this next test."

The white coat nodded and continued their examination while Alex held his breath, anticipating what was to come.

The General clenched his hands with excitement as he addressed the crowd in the room. "Excellent!" he exclaimed, rubbing his palms together. "Do you know what this means? We are the first to have successfully revived and re-animated a corpse. We will be funded for as long as we can work, which will mean a raise for all of you."

Cheers reverberated through the lab as the assistants high-fived each other, smiles spreading across their faces like wildfire. Alex looked around from his spot on the table, trying to take in the overwhelming joy radiating from everyone, but he couldn't see them all from where he was strapped.

The General stepped back from the table and gestured to a taller female assistant in a tight white lab coat. She leaned over Alex and injected an abnormally long needle into the left side of his forehead. Pain flooded Alex's head, and he struggled to breathe and think as a fog spread across his brain and his eyes began to burn. He felt himself drift off into the darkness before being jolted awake.

Alex sat straight up, feeling for his forehead and then running his fingers over his eyes. Relief washed over him when he realized he wasn't in the lab anymore, no longer with an oversized needle jabbed in his skull. It had all been a dream... no a memory. He never left the house. He had remembered something so real that it almost explained why his mom thought he had died – he must've gone somewhere else between then and now. But where?

Alex's heart raced as two car engines echoed outside the small bedroom window. Dogkey stood on his hind legs, watching the scene through slightly parted curtains.

As Alex stood to get a better look, he saw two white vans had stopped outside the house. Several men in navy blue suits and dark sunglasses stepped out and scanned the area. All of them looked similar with identical haircuts. Could these be the federal agents the sheriff mentioned?

The men began to talk, their voices low but distinct enough for Alex and Dogkey to pick up what they were saying. A man pulled out a map and said, "Agent Lee, this is the last house for five miles. Based on their time until sunrise, they would probably be here if they're heading south."

"That's what you've said about the last six houses," Agent Lee answered gruffly.

"We just know that they would have stopped, sir. We don't know how fast they traveled or if they waited until the last possible light. It's largely based on guesswork."

Agent Lee sighed before asking, "Let's assume they did wait until the last light and ran fast - are there any more places after this one that they could possibly be hiding in?"

"Not that we have found, sir."

Agent Lee gritted his teeth and slammed the van door shut.

Alex could hear faint footsteps drawing closer through the house's open windows. He spun around to look at Dogkey and saw the large claws extending from his hands. He imitated a swipe through the air before pointing at his nails again, but Alex shook his head firmly. "No! I said no more killing. We fight only as a last resort. There has to be another way".

Dogkey reluctantly nodded, and Alex left the room and quickly searched the kitchen for somewhere to hide. His eyes landed on a small door, barely bigger than the refrigerator beside it. He rushed over and tried to open the handle but found it locked tight.

Alex tugged on the doorknob and was met with a rusted squeal as it opened, revealing a closet large enough to fit him and Dogkey. His gaze shifted between the door and the refrigerator across from them in the kitchen, and a plan formed in his head. He grabbed Dogkey's paw and rushed towards the kitchen, babbling. "When we're inside the closet, reach out and pull this fridge towards us," he gestured to the appliance.

Dogkey nodded, stepping inside. Alex followed suit, and the creature pulled the fridge in front of their hiding spot, partially blocking their hiding spot with the refrigerator. No one would guess there was a door behind it.

The house's front door creaked open, and two agents stepped inside carefully. The duo searched every corner of the room, not sparing even an empty box or broken furniture piece. With each area checked off their list, they congregated in the kitchen.

"Did you find anything?" One questioned, his voice echoing off of the walls.

"Nothing," the other replied. "The house is empty."

"Lee is going to be very upset."

"You're telling me," grumbled the first man, taking a map from his pocket. "I'm sure he'll blame me for this." He motioned for them all to leave, palpable despair hovering in their wake.

Alex heard the sound of boots scuffing on the hardwood floor and muffled male voices as the men shuffled out of the house. He tensed as he listened for the slam of the door, which eventually came and left an eerie silence in its wake. The air was thick and close inside the closet, tinged with dust and sweat. A part of him craved fresh air, but Alex knew better than to risk it. If they stayed put, there would be less chance of being discovered. He motioned for his friend to sit next to him on the bare floorboards as they huddled together in wait until nightfall again.

CHAPTER TWENTY-FIVE

Sheriff McCoo slammed the receiver down on the phone jack, running a hand through his thinning gray hair. His pale complexion drained of the last traces of color.

The baby-faced Deputy stepped closer, hesitating before finally asking, "What did they say?"

McCoo sighed heavily, "The State Police aren't sending anyone; because of budget cuts, they are short on men and told me to call the Feds for help."

Doctor Wilbur Williams, who had been standing off in the corner, spoke up. "You mean we are on our own. Right?"

McCoo shook his head slowly. The six deputies exchanged worried glances as the Sheriff said, "No. This town needs the law, and I wouldn't feel right if any of you got hurt over this...I'm going alone."

He pointed at various puddles of blood and evidence scattered across the floor as he continued, "I want you guys to stay here, I will call you if I need something, but otherwise, this will be my operation."

But Doctor Wilbur Williams didn't miss a beat. He stepped closer and firmly declared, "I will go with you then. If nothing else, to watch your back or help if you get hurt. And knowing you, I expect that there will be at least one injury you will need to be treated."

McCoo's fiery blue eyes locked with the Doctor's kind hazel ones as he argued, "Absolutely not. You are a civilian, and besides, don't you have a lot of work to do here?"

Doc squared his shoulders and looked the sheriff in the eye. He stared at him for a few seconds to get a read on his friend. "They're loading the last of the bodies into the wagon below, and we both know how these men died. I'd normally perform forensics on this case, but it's unnecessary here. So no, I don't have anything to do. There's no reason I can't go."

The sheriff hesitated before reluctantly replying, "Fine. But you better mind me, or I'll leave you by the roadside."

"Agreed," Doc replied with a crisp salute. "Sir!"

"Lovely."

Agent Lee entered the laboratory, his gaze scanning for the project leader. He soon spotted a scar-faced man bent over a microscope and hurried across the room toward him. He gently tapped the shoulder and said, "General, we have been unable to locate the Chromosome 19 subjects, but there's a place we think they'll be headed."

The General's face flushed crimson with rage, and his fists clenched as he struggled to control his temper. He knew that the agent subjects were hostile to verbal outbursts and, in some ways, were like his sons. Taking a deep breath, he asked calmly, "Are there any structures along that route or elsewhere where we could undertake further experiments?"

"There is a house, sir," Agent Lee replied.

A smile crept onto the General's face as he rubbed his hands together eagerly. "Good. Follow me."

He led Agent Lee to one of the experiment doors and slid open a hatch on its surface. Motioning for Agent Lee to look inside, he asked, "What do you see?"

Agent Lee peered into the darkness, and after a few seconds, he noticed dozens of tiny red eyes staring back at him from within. "All I can see are lots of tiny red eyes in there," he whispered.

He leaned into the open cargo hatch, watching the General's experiment emerge. Foot-long creatures that were half rat and half-shark scurried out of the crates, all deformed in some fashion. They moved quickly, almost frantically, as if searching for something.

"These are my latest development," the General said, voice full of pride. "I was able to affect the rat animal cell and transfer the genes of a shark. As you will see, they will provide quick and efficient results."

The creatures were still searching as Agent Lee asked, "Are you sure they will go after the boy and his pet?"

"They are bred with a strong scent for the dog/monkey creature," the General replied. "I had them test with him in the field area, and they have his scent. If the boy has touched the beast, he will be subject to my attack pets."

Agent Lee nodded before asking, "And how exactly would you round them up."

"You don't have to worry about it," The General said dismissively. "When the sun comes up, they will die, and those that made it to shelter will eventually get caught in the light. I have plenty here, so the loss will not be a problem."

The General looked into the open hatch and smiled. "Soon, my pets. Soon, you will be able to eat."

CHAPTER TWENTY-SIX

FBI West Coast Headquarters

San Francisco, California

FBI Western Regional Deputy Director shook hands with Special Agent Brian Trudy at the door of his large office and gestured for him to enter. Trudy could feel the anticipation building as he noticed they were not alone in the room. The room was decorated in mauve, dark mahogany furniture and smelled faintly of leather and gun oil.

In one corner, a small balding man perched on the edge of a couch clutching a tablet and pen, while another grey-haired man that he knew by appearance to be George Block, seated in front of the Deputy Director's massive desk, almost blended into the background. Special Agent Wertz, Trudy assumed to be his new partner, gave him an unamused nod from the couch across the room. He wanted to argue that he didn't need a partner but kept silent as he noticed the Deputy Director sizing him up.

Trudy handed the Deputy Director a two-inch thick manila folder with no labels before easing himself into one of the plush armchairs facing the desk. The Deputy Director opened it slowly, revealing pages filled with strange symbols and diagrams. "This is the journal of General Lawrence," he read as he flipped through it. "The purpose of this is to track each experiment and my success. Each section is designed to report on a different subject. Section one covers the cloning process."

The Deputy Director looked perplexed and said, "I thought we were funding a BWMD project, not cloning. Where is the funding for cloning experiments?"

Agent Wertz shook his head. "The intel we've gathered says that the General has gone rogue, veering further from our plan than we had intended. Is he trying to create a modern-day Frankenstein?"

Wertz's inquiry sent Agent Trudy into a whirlwind of indignation, quickly silenced by the Deputy Director's throat-clearing.

"There's no use getting angry, Agent Trudy. It's an honest question. Do we have proof that he could meet his deadline and deliver on his promise?"

Trudy nodded resolutely. "I can guarantee it, sir. I've been pushing him hard and know for certain that he'll be finished in two weeks. I even visited the site myself and saw the creatures working firsthand. It was remarkable. I reminded him, though, that if he failed to fulfill the task, I'd pull all funding for the project."

The Deputy Director scoured through the reports before handing them back to Trudy. "I can't make out anything from this mess of science jargon; care to explain what exactly he's doing?"

Trudy navigated his way through the folder until he found a year-old report. He cleared his throat before beginning to read aloud.

"May 1st, I attempted to create the first creature through somatic cell manipulation. Carefully adding genes to the existing cells of a gorilla's body, I hoped for success in taking on canine traits. But the experiment had failed, like that of a teenager from the University of Pennsylvania in 1990: May 15th, another unsuccessful merger between two grown species. Frustrated, I set out to find a different approach.

"This is all very interesting," the Deputy Director said. "But it still doesn't tell me how he is creating these biological weapons."

"There's more," Trudy said, flipping a few pages. "June 1st brought tremendous results; instead of looking for a quick fix, I injected an embryonic stem cell from a dog into the egg cell of a monkey and followed up with standard germline manipulation. I merged canine and simian DNA with a promoter control sequence, creating a creature that could pass the combined genes onto its offspring. Although this creature may not be what we need, its descendants will undoubtedly be.

"Let me get this straight," the Deputy Director said, his brow furrowing. "Instead of creating the creature we need, he created its parent. That doesn't make sense - it would take years to accomplish such a feat."

"Not exactly," Trudy replied nervously. "He goes on. The introduction of the advanced development techniques I used on my clones has sped up the fetus development process." He paused and brushed a lock of hair from his face before continuing. "The construct containing one strand of DNA from the monkey and one strand of DNA from the dog is alive and will soon reach adulthood. I have already begun to modify its plasmids to allow its offspring to have the specific traits I wanted in the first place. Now, I can experiment with other combinations, but this method has been set in motion - merge two species' DNAs together so that traits can be passed down to future generations and then slightly enhance them to create what I need."

The Assistant Director was incredulous. "And that's the experiment that we're expecting?"

Trudy nodded slowly. "As soon as he retrieves it..." he trailed off, realizing a moment too late what he had just said.

"Retrieves it?" The Assistant Director asked, turning expectantly towards the Deputy Director. "What does that mean?"

Trudy cleared his throat uncomfortably. "During a test, it escaped, sir," he explained quickly. "But he should have it soon enough."

The Deputy Director's eyes narrowed further, and he leaned forward. "Is that why I've got a Sheriff from the town near your site? They're asking questions about our agents hunting down some boy?"

"It is connected, sir."

Agent Wertz slowly rose from the couch, his eyes on the ground as he walked towards the Deputy Director's desk. The man's face was flushed, and veins bulged at his temples, making his presence known without a word. "We have the Montana facility ready," Wertz said, attempting to break through the tension in the air. "We could relocate the project there."

The Deputy Director slammed his fist on the desk and pointed directly at Agent Trudy. "You get down there," he bellowed. "And make sure the Sheriff isn't trying to investigate this Department! We already have those inquiries from him."

"I don't have to tell you those are from the General's Blue Agent Project. No real agents were sent." The Deputy Director's voice was an angry whisper before continuing in a lower octave. "You know what? I don't care. I want you and Wertz to get a handle on this, or you will have some personal problems. And tell that mad scientist to get a handle on his experiments, or it will be his neck. Am I completely understood?"

Agent Trudy nodded silently and quickly left the room, followed by Wertz a few moments later.

CHAPTER
TWENTY-SEVEN

Holiday Inn, Room 119

San Francisco, California

Agent Trudy sat cross-legged on his hotel room bed. The contents of the two files he received from the Deputy Director's secretary were scattered all around him. He had returned from his meeting at precisely half past six and had spent the last thirty minutes organizing the materials dealing with the Goldpan enigma into three separate stacks.

Trudy reached down and picked up the first group of papers on his left. The little yellow post-it note he had placed on it read, 'Geographical Layout.' Among other things, the stack contained a map of Goldpan and the surrounding mountain areas. He cocked his head to the right and turned the map slightly to view the town from the point he would enter. He quickly surveyed the map and saw something that concerned him. There was only one road into the city, and if there had been an incident in Goldpan, that single road could be a severe problem for escape. It did lead out to the main highway. From there, any escapee could head anywhere in the desert or beyond.

He committed the town layout to memory and the roads leading into the nearby mountains and flipped the paper over. On the back of the map was a timetable listing the forecasted sunrise and sundown for the next two weeks. He also committed the timetable to memory and spent a few minutes reviewing the other papers in his hands; the materials listed topographical information and elevation numbers. Satisfied that he had thoroughly studied the first group, he set the stack in his open briefcase on the night table and picked up the second stack.

The second group's yellow Post-it note read, 'Review and Detail of Incident to Date.' He briefly read over the three pages in this stack, searching for any detail from the Sheriff's transcribed complaints and questions. He needed to get a handle on where to focus first for damage control. Maybe something the Deputy Director could have unintentionally left out of the debriefing. He couldn't put his finger on precisely what it was, but he was sure his superior had held something back during their talk. He nodded, read the report, and decided he had been told every last detail. He reread the report just to be sure and still found nothing new. As with the first group, he placed this report into his briefcase.

Trudy grabbed the final stack and looked at its yellow note; it read, 'Internal Confidential Informant Report.' The first sheet outlined the background of the contact. It described his role and connections. This didn't interest him much, so he moved on to the second sheet.

The subsequent papers in the stack listed all of the mole's reports. For the most part, they mirrored what the General had told him, but with one exception. The information was filled with many details about the Sheriff and his department. He couldn't be sure, but the informant almost sounded like he admired McCoo.

"I guess I should reach out to this guy," Trudy said out loud.

He skimmed through the other sheets of information on the standard capacity and capabilities of the local law enforcement. He came across a page with a red stamped 'Confidential' on the top. He quickly returned the paper to the bottom of the stack. It wasn't meant for his eyes.

He set the third set of papers in his briefcase and stood to stretch. He bent down, touched his toes, raised upright, and bent down again. He looked down at the briefcase as he exercised, and a voice echoed through his mind, ordering him to read the confidential memo. He raised his arms above his head and bent his hands back until they cracked. He sighed with relief and then turned his torso sideways until his back made a similar cracking sound. His eyes had remained focused on the papers the entire time.

"My gut tells me to read it," Trudy said to himself.

He rummaged through the top stack of papers and produced the seductive memo. His eyes passed over the confidential warning and darted to the body of the letter. It was a short memo and had only two paragraphs. It read:

Under Doctor Michaels, the second location is proceeding with no delays. Agent Wertz appears to manage things to the task. We will assign him to Agent Trudy to help the struggling operative.

From our experiments, the Montana location has shown a bond between the child and the creature. It is most likely true for Goldpan. We have withheld the information from the agent even though it might help them recapture it. We want to see how the experiment proceeds without the agent's predisposition or knowledge.

Trudy stopped reading. He was staring at the last sentence he read.

He kicked the bed, angry that information had been withheld from him and they thought him struggling. He had been with the Bureau enough years to be treated as a seasoned operative and didn't need a damn babysitter, but withholding information was the worst. Over the years, he had learned to trust his gut instinct, and in this case, it was plain to see that his gut was about the only thing he would be able to trust.

Deputy Director George Block sluggishly shuffled down the cold, brightly lit corridor. With each click of his hard-soled shoe on the shiny tile floor, his head pounded in agony. He had spent most of the previous night at the local tavern, and like always, he had drunk himself into oblivion. As he reached the door to his office, he instinctively reached into his pocket and searched for the key.

Block slid the key into the hole, the metal against metal sound echoing through his cranium. He fumbled against the wall next to the entrance with his sweaty palm until he found the light switch. Softly he flipped it on. He opened the door, oozed into the office, and gently shut the door behind him.

"Good morning." Agent Trudy said in a strong, firm voice.

Block's eyes glared across the room at the man sitting behind his desk. He was both surprised and angry to see the agent in his office.

"How the hell did you get in here?" said Block in the angriest voice he could muster after such a draining evening.

Trudy's eyes smiled at Block as he responded, "I'm a trained FBI Agent. Do you think that a small lock would hold me out of your office?"

"What are you doing in here? Your butt should be on its way to Goldpan. If you think that you can…"

"First off," interrupted Trudy. "I'm not due to leave for Goldpan for another hour. As for what I'm doing here, we need to talk." He motioned for Block to sit in the chair in front of the desk as the Deputy Director had done in his office at their earlier meeting.

"Get out from behind my desk," he ordered in a rage.

Smiling from ear to ear, Trudy stood from the chair and sat on the corner of Block's desk. "As you wish," he said sarcastically.

"I don't know what you learned in the Academy, but my position warrant's a little respect from the likes of you," bellowed Block as he wobbled to his chair and dropped to its firm cushion.

"Respect," Trudy exclaimed with a chuckle, "How about the respect an Agent deserves."

"What the hell are you talking about?"

"You know damn well what I'm talking about, sir," Trudy said, straining his voice on the last word. "I deserved to know about the other location and experiments."

Block's eyes inflated to the size of golf balls. In an instant, Fern was sure that his superior knew what he was referring to. Block shifted in his seat and cleared his throat. His back was against the wall. He looked at Trudy and thought for a moment. He had an obligation to tell the agent about the memo, but he knew keeping it from him had been a good idea. He could feign ignorance to mislead the young man but decided to be truthful.

"How did you find out?" Block reluctantly asked.

"There was a copy of the memo in my review package, and Wertz mentions Montana in the Deputy Director's office."

"And it furnished the reasons," Block mumbled, finishing Trudy's sentence.

Trudy then asked, "Why didn't you tell me? Or why didn't you at least mention another location, for that matter."

"We," Block stopped himself and corrected his error. "I thought it would be best if you didn't know. I felt it could jeopardize the mission."

"Not knowing is a bigger jeopardy."

"I suppose I could see that."

"Tell me all the details, and I won't report the fact that there was evidence withheld from me on a federal investigation."

Block swallowed hard and explained the other location and the different experiments to Trudy. Trudy listened closely, intrigued. When Block finished, he thanked him and walked towards the office door.

" Hey, kid," Block called.

"Yes."

"Be careful."

Trudy smiled as he stepped out of the Assistant Director's office. "Thank you, sir. I will."

Block waited until Trudy closed the door behind him before he reached into his desk drawer. He pulled out a shot glass and a bottle of whiskey. He was disgusted with himself. He had melted in Trudy's hands. His defenses had peeled away, and a bitter old man had answered the questions.

He picked up the whiskey and stared at the half-full demon. The bottle in his shaking hand filled the shot glass without spilling a drop. He raised the glass to his lips. "Here's to Goldpan," Block said as he jerked his head back, swallowing the contents of the tiny glass. He placed the glass back on his desk and filled it again.

CHAPTER TWENTY-EIGHT

Dogkey and Alex had escaped. The boy slowly rose to his feet in the pitch black, stretching out the stiffness that had settled into his limbs from hours cramped together. His companion's large eyes glowed a luminous red next to him, and a wave of comfort rippled through Alex.

Gesturing towards the door, he said softly, "Let's go. I think it has been long enough by now." Dogkey silently nodded and curled one of its claws around the handle, pushing against the door with a creak of protest as if it were reluctant to let them escape. Straining hard, Dogkey finally managed to shift the heavy refrigerator blocking their path just enough for them to slip through. As the metal legs scraped harshly against the floor, Alex felt his spine tingle with apprehension.

Once out of the closet, Alex entered the kitchen and surveyed the sky outside. He smiled in relief when he saw that night had blanketed all but the faintest edges of sunset, providing enough darkness for them to move about unnoticed. "Just in time," he commented, turning to Dogkey, still lingering by the door frame. "Ready?"

Dogkey didn't move.

Alex extended a reassuring hand, beckoning his companion forward. "It's okay, Dogkey, come on. We can do this."

The creature stood in the dark closet, trembling. Alex slowly stepped in, waving his hands and attempting to soothe the scared monster. "It's okay," he said softly, repeating himself repeatedly. "Come on. You got this."

When Dogkey finally emerged from the hiding place, Alex could see his body was stiff with fear, expecting the lab of evil men in white coats to wait for him.

Alex climbed onto the back of his friend. He adjusted himself and tapped Dogkey on the shoulder. "I think I got a good grip. Let's get going."

Dogkey attempted to open the door before him, scratching at the wood around the handle with his sharp claws as he struggled to twist the doorknob. Finally, it opened, revealing the darkness of night beyond their safe haven. They galloped out into its depths and headed south into the desert.

They traveled continuously for six hours, Dogkey pushing through despite growing fatigue. Alex could feel his friend tiring beneath him, but Dogkey would never admit it; instead, he remained stoic and silent to protect Alex from harm.

To his left, Alex noticed a two-story house with a bright red barn perched regally behind it, and his heart leaped with excitement at the sight. The creature carrying him had been running for hours through treacherous terrain, and he wanted to do something to give the soft-hearted mix-breed some relief. He had been looking for an excuse to take a break from the long journey, and this seemed like the perfect spot.

"I need to rest," Alex lied in Dogkey's ear as he heard the creature's breathing become more ragged. "There is a barn over there. Can we please go in there and rest a little while?"

Alex could feel Dogkey sigh in relief and nod before changing direction and trotting toward the house and barn. As they got closer to the home, both friends saw a large car parked in the driveway by the front of the house, raising their suspicions. Still, they cautiously approached the open barn door until they were safely inside.

Dogkey lifted Alex off his back and laid him in the hay as he stretched and dropped to the ground next to him. Alex studied his surroundings - taking in all the dried grass - and marveled at how much hay there was in one place. He figured that whoever owned this house must have quite a few horses, though it was strange that none were present at this hour.

"You rest," Alex said, standing up and walking around the barn. "I will keep watching for a little while."

Dogkey didn't argue but closed his eyes and drifted off. Alex, who wasn't tired from the ride, patted his friend on the head and stepped out into the night air. He looked up to the top floor of the house and scanned the darkened windows, wondering who lived there and if there were children inside. He studied the surrounding area for signs of danger.

Strolling towards the car parked fifty or so feet away, he noticed something different about it in the moonlight - its passenger side window had been smashed in. Peering inside, he gasped in horror. There was part of a man lying across the front seats. It appeared that something had taken several large bites out of him. The expression on the corpse's face was sheer terror, indicating that this person died very afraid of whatever creature had attacked them. There were no claw marks. That meant it couldn't have been Dogkey. What else had escaped?

Alex backed away slowly, sickened by what he had seen.

The deserted farmhouse seemed to hold some dark secret, but Alex couldn't tell if the danger was inside or outside. His heart pounded in his chest, and he felt as though menacing shadows surrounded him like a thousand eyes were watching. He glanced at the barn, then back at the house again—should he get Dogkey or investigate the house on his own?

He decided that if someone needed help, he should take it upon himself to see what was wrong. Taking an unsteady breath to steel himself, Alex walked towards the house. He debated whether or not to call for Dogkey. He didn't want to bother him if he was resting, but he needed all the courage he could get. When he reached the porch steps, Alex noticed for the first time that the front door was slightly open, its frame splintered from being busted in.

Gripping his flashlight tightly, Alex stepped over the threshold and entered the house. The door's hinges let out a piercing creak as if nails were being dragged across a chalkboard. The skin on his neck prickled, and his heart raced faster. With trepidation, he swallowed hard and pushed further into the house.

Alex stopped in the living room doorframe, his eyes scanning the area. The furniture was arranged neatly, a soft tan couch and armchair facing a large flat-screen television. Magazines were scattered across the coffee table, with titles ranging from Outdoor Living to DIY Home Improvement Projects. Moonlight streamed through the window, highlighting freshly vacuumed carpet and dust-free surfaces. Nothing seemed out of place, yet something felt off. There was no sign of life in this home. Was the only occupant the unfortunate dead man out in the car?"

"Hello, is anyone here?" His voice echoed off the walls as he called out into the emptiness. He moved cautiously from room to room on the first floor, searching for anything that might tell him someone else had passed through recently.

He stopped in the kitchen, his stomach growling at the sight of the refrigerator stocked with food. Alex couldn't help but smile as he grabbed a few apples for Dogkey and peeled back foil from several dishes revealing leftover turkey legs, mashed potatoes, and steamed vegetables.

"Mind if I have something to eat?" Again, there was no response, only silence. He let it linger momentarily before softly saying, "Thank you."

He had been depriving himself of meat for so long that he couldn't believe how delicious it was. Bringing it to his mouth, he took the most considerable bite his mouth could give him and let the savory flavor of the turkey flood his taste buds. He savored each bite more than the last, then grabbed the milk carton and greedily guzzled from it.

CRASH! CRASH! CRASH!

The sudden banging sound from upstairs frightened him, causing him to choke on the milk in surprise. His heart raced as he heard little feet scurrying across the floorboards above him. It sounded like hundreds of cats running.

Alex hastily set down the unfinished meal and hurried towards the staircase, chasing after the strange noise. The light from the open refrigerator door illuminated his path up the carpeted steps. Once he reached the halfway point between floors, he struggled to get a better view of what was happening upstairs. But the short ceiling prevented him from seeing anything, so he grasped onto the railing and climbed the stairs until he reached the second story. Everything looked in place and seemed normal, but Alex still couldn't shake off an eerie feeling.

"Hello, I need some help for a man out front," Alex said softly. His voice echoed down the hallway, and he held his breath while waiting for a response. He couldn't shake the feeling that someone was watching him as he nervously grasped the handle to the first door on his right. With a gentle push, the door opened silently, revealing a messy bedroom. The room was cold but not empty. Alex felt an unease settle in his gut as he surveyed the disheveled bed sheets and wondered who could've slept in such a mess.

Suddenly, his speculation was interrupted by a loud crash further down the hall, prompting him to rush toward the sound with a pounding heart. Pushing open the next door with his foot, Alex found himself face-to-face with disarray. Broken vases lay scattered across the floor, and shelves were overturned with books strewn everywhere. Fearfully, he crept into the room, expecting someone or something to jump out at him.

Alex approached the door to the bathroom, and when he peered inside, he noticed the distinct smell of bleach permeating the air. He stepped into the room and looked around warily. To his right, a flowered shower curtain hung high above the tub, revealing any possible hiding spot behind it. On his left, the toilet lid was back against its tank at attention as if waiting for Alex's inspection. The room was clean. When he found no one present, he cautiously exited the room and started down the hall.

Suddenly, a crashing sound rang out from behind him, and Alex spun around in alarm. He retraced his steps back to the bathroom door, but this time it was closed. Something or someone had gone inside and shut it after them. His heart pounded in fear. Alex pushed open the door and stepped into the bathroom again. This time, however, the toilet lid was now down. With trembling hands, he gripped it tightly and slowly opened it up. Nothing seemed out of place...until he raised his head to the ceiling.

There, perched on top of an air vent, was a small creature with four legs and deep red eyes staring straight at Alex. Its head was nearly twice as large as its body, and its long tail curled around a metal bracket that held it in place. It let out a menacing growl as its four rows of razor-sharp teeth glinted eerily in the light. Alex knew this had to be one of the General's creations. It matched perfectly with those strange bite marks he had seen on the man outside earlier. Fear coursed through Alex's veins as he realized this creature had been responsible for all this chaos.

Smiling nervously, Alex's eyes widened, and his breath quickened. The red-eyed creature kept baring its teeth atop the ceiling as if ready to pounce. Every step he took was echoed by the predator, making it impossible to reach the door. His hands were trembling now as adrenaline surged through him. Noticing his escape route closing off, Alex quickly lunged for the door handle and yanked it shut behind him. He heard a loud thud and felt the door vibrate a second after locking it. He imagined the creature running head-on into the hardwood, causing a momentary thought of humor from a cartoon.

He wanted out of this house more than ever before. If this monster was here, there had to be more. When he saw two of them scurrying up the stairs from the first floor, he panicked and quickly backstepped down the hall until his back bumped against a door at the end. Fumbling with the handle, he flung himself inside and shut the door behind him.

Resting his head on the door, Alex let out a sigh of relief and turned around. His throat went dry, and he found it hard to breathe as the sickly-sweet, smell of death hit his nostrils. In the center of the room, hundreds of small rat-like creatures had taken over a large bed, their black fur contrasting starkly with the white sheets. They yipped and squeaked in excitement, their tiny red eyes glittering with malicious glee as they feasted on the two dark shapes at the center of the bed.

Alex took an involuntary step back, turning just in time to see more monsters filing into the hallway from every direction. They had cut off his escape routes like trained operatives. There was nowhere to run - these ravenous little beasts surrounded him on all sides. He could hear them hungrily clicking their razor-sharp teeth together, craving more flesh to consume.

Desperate, Alex scurried towards a window at the far side of the room, but his path was quickly blocked as more creatures clambered through the opening. He paused in dismay, realizing there was no way to escape this horror - these merciless monsters completely trapped him. Taking a deep breath, he muttered a quiet "Oh no" under his breath.

CHAPTER TWENTY-NINE

The squad car drove on, its headlights cutting through the darkness of the desert. It had been an hour since Sheriff McCoo and Doctor Williams left the main road, and neither one had spoken a word. The tension in the car was almost tangible, with both men wide awake and scared for what they might find.

"What exactly are we looking for?" Doc Williams asked, breaking the silence.

"What do you mean?" Sheriff McCoo replied.

"Why are we driving out here in the middle of nowhere? You left the main road a half hour ago, and we haven't seen so much as a coyote since then. So, I want to know what we are looking for out here."

"The same thing as before, Doc. I am after the kid, and if that creature is with him. I want justice for my boys back in the room."

Sheriff McCoo glanced at the desolate landscape surrounding them, rolling hills of dry gray dirt dotted with sparse patches of hardy desert plants and shrubs stretching endlessly into the horizon. He shifted uncomfortably in his seat before continuing, "When I was listening to Agent Lee talk to his men, it was mentioned that the boy was heading directly south. If so, I can follow a straight line in that direction and run into them."

Doc nodded slowly, shifting in his passenger seat. He looked around at their surroundings before hesitating, "But I need to use the bathroom, and out in the middle of the desert, I don't have anywhere to go."

Sheriff McCoo glanced at Doc sympathetically; "I'll pull over, and you can go behind a tree." He remembered their fishing trips together when Doc refused to venture into any wilderness setting due to his city upbringing.

Doc chuckled slightly. "Do you not remember our last two wilderness adventures? I can't go in the woods anymore. I guess it must be that city boy in me."

The sheriff smiled faintly before returning his gaze to the long stretch ahead; "Yeah, your right." He paused briefly before adding softly, "How long have we known each other, Doc?"

Doc placed his hand on his friend's shoulder and exhaled deeply. He could smell the faintest hint of cigarettes on him, months-old nicotine patches still clinging to his clothes. "Going on almost ten years, I would guess. Why do you ask?"

"It's just that you are the closest thing I have to family around here. And if something happened to me, I'm not sure who would be there to bury me. I just wanted to..."

"Whoa there," Doc replied, raising his hands in defense. He looked up at the starlit sky for a moment before continuing. "In all these years, you have never even brought this up. Is there something you want to talk about, or maybe something I don't know?"

"I'm just not sure how this will turn out. And if it goes bad, I want to ensure that things are taken care of, you know?"

Doc nodded slowly and gestured towards the road ahead, crossing the offroad path in front of them. The squad car creaked as they turned onto the paved road, and he glanced at his friend with an unwavering gaze. "First off, nothing is going to go bad. Second, you are talking to the wrong person. If something goes bad, I'm with you. I doubt I'd be much better at planning your funeral if I died too."

His friend chuckled lightly before speaking again. "Good point. If there's any shooting, I'd suggest that you duck."

"Not that I am bored by the conversation," Doc said before quickly changing gears, "but could we please detour and find a gas station?"

"Sure, but only this once," his old friend jested halfheartedly. "If you have to go again, I'm going to start thinking you don't want me to find this kid."

The truck slowed, and Doc threw his friend a questioning look. "That was an odd thing to say." Doctor Williams peered closely at him, concern furrowing his brows as he spoke again. "Don't you trust me?"

Heaving a weighted sigh, McCoo steered onto the highway and answered quietly, "Of course I do. I just told you we were like family." After a beat of silence, he added more forcefully, "You should get some rest. The lack of sleep is making you a little crazy."

The Doctor smiled and nodded at the Sheriff's words, but his tight-lipped expression betrayed his apprehension. He turned back towards the road, searching for a sign of bathroom hope.

A few moments later, Sheriff McCoo pointed ahead with a triumphant grin. "Look, Doc! I-5 winds around so much that we ran into the road again. And there is that gas station you were hoping for!"

Sure enough, the bright neon lights of a newer gas station illuminated the night sky. The Sheriff pulled his car to a stop before the wooden garage doors, and Doc Williams quickly got out to investigate. As he returned from around the corner a moment later, he clutched a large piece of wood with a key attached. With newfound excitement in his step, he disappeared around back.

CHAPTER THIRTY

Alex huddled against the wall, his body tense with anticipation. He was as defenseless as he'd felt in his nightmares of the lab and the scar-faced general. Clenching his fists tight, he muttered a prayer and braced himself. The tiny creatures with large sharp teeth moved closer.

Suddenly, the glass next to him broke into a hundred pieces, and Dogkey bounded through the window, powerful paws crushing some of the tiny creatures on the floor beneath him. The mutants turned their attention to him with angry shrieks. In fives, they launched themselves at Dogkey, mouths wide open, with small teeth clamping onto whatever part of him they could sink into.

Dogkey roared as he frantically tried to remove the little monsters latched on his skin. They had latched on like leeches and wouldn't let go, no matter how hard he shook them off. With one final tug, clumps of hair ripped away in their mouths before they fell to the ground.

The creature flung more rodents across the room and stomped on any that reached him with sharp claws, but there were just too many for one half-dog, half-monkey being to fend off. Soon they would overtake him, leaving Alex on his own. He couldn't let that happen.

Alex yelled in alarm, and Dogkey felt the same terror course through him. He could feel the tiny creatures scuttling up his body, moving closer and closer to ending his life. Reacting quickly, Dogkey scooped Alex onto his back and leaped out the window. They sailed toward the ground as Dogkey frantically shook off any monsters clinging to him. With a loud thud, they hit the earth, beating their pursuers by seconds.

Alex climbed off, patting Dogkey on the back in gratitude. Dogkey looked up at the window, watching anxiously for any sign of pursuit before finally relaxing. Dropping down onto his bottom, he started scrabbling in the dirt at his feet. Alex leaned over and smiled when he read what Dogkey had written – 'Welcome.' Dogkey continued writing, forming two words - 'Shrats' and 'Light'. Alex paused, confusion etched into his face before asking what Dogkey meant by going into the light. Dogkey nodded, and Alex realized he was referring to sunlight - the only thing stopping this deadly half-shark, half-rat creature.

Dogkey leaped to his feet, his eyes zeroing in on the house's second-story window they had been hiding in. Alex followed the creature's gaze and watched, horrified, as wave after wave of Shrats tumbled out of the window and down the side of the house. More than what they had initially seen, these creatures were relentless and fast, quickly gaining ground on their prey. With no time to lose, Dogkey backed away from the edge of a small valley only yards away, lowering himself to the ground in a sprinter's stance. Alex clambered onto his back with arms around his neck, unsure why they had stopped running.

"What are you doing?" he yelled over the roar of chasing Shrats. "Why have we stopped? They're almost here!"

Dogkey waited for the creatures to get closer. Satisfied, he ran towards the valley, his legs pumping with all the strength he could muster. Alex watched as his companion leaped from the cliff's edge and soared through the air for an eternity. When Dogkey finally landed on the other side, Alex's breath caught in his throat. The little monster's shrill cries echoed behind them, but Dogkey had put enough distance between them to give Alex time to think.

Dogkey continued running until they reached a road. He cautiously crossed it and moved a few feet away, glancing up and down its length before turning southward again. As he pushed forward, Alex could tell that Dogkey was slowing down from exhaustion. But no matter how hard he tried, their pursuers were still catching up. What could they do?

CHAPTER THIRTY-ONE

Alex squinted as he watched the morning sun's red glow rise, spreading its light and heat across the land like a blanket. As the brilliant hue swept across the desert landscape, Alex was surprised to see hundreds of small dark shapes scatter in a panic, their screams of terror piercing the air. He sensed Dogkey's body tense up from the brightness and heard him whimper in pain.

The sight of the roasting Shrats brought a smile to his face, but it quickly faded as he noticed Dogkey's fur smoking and charring from the intense heat. Dropping to his knees beside Dogkey, Alex hesitated briefly before gathering his strength to help his friend stand. "Come on, you have to get up," he said firmly yet kindly. "We have to keep going, or you could die."

Dogkey's feet scraped against the pavement as he attempted to stand, but his paws gave out, and he fell heavily to the ground again. Alex rushed over to him and placed a comforting hand on his side, willing him to get back up. With Alex's help, Dogkey lurched forward clumsily, only making it a few steps before collapsing again.

Tears pooled in Alex's eyes, and he begged, "You have to get up. Please don't leave me."

At that moment, there was a flurry of noise as a light brown sheriff's car skidded to a stop beside them. Both doors flung open, and Sheriff McCoo stepped out with gun drawn. He sternly commanded Alex to move away from Dogkey while Doctor Williams approached cautiously in scrubs and a white coat.

Alex shouted in desperation, "Are you crazy? Put that gun away! This is my friend, and he's hurt. I need your help. Are you a doctor?" pointing towards the overweight Doc Williams.

Doc Williams replied, "I am, but I don't know what to do for that animal. I'm not even sure what it is."

"It's my friend," insisted Alex, anxiously tugging at his clothes, "He needs our help. The sun is burning him. Please help me get him out of the light, or he will die!"

"From what I've seen of its handiwork, that would be good. He tore a lot of fine men up. I lost people who were my friends, and my deputies have been taken away from their families. I say if the sun can kill it, then let it die," Sheriff McCoo said, holstering his gun. "It may not be dangerous now, but we shouldn't take the chance that it might be later."

"Please," Alex pleaded, laying his body across Dogkey to block the sun. His body was too small and made no difference in stopping the cooking of his hairy friend. "He was trying to protect me from the guys that hurt us. He didn't understand the difference between the men who did the experiments and those who were nice to me. They all look alike to him. But he does know now he won't hurt anyone. I promise."

"Maybe we should help it. If nothing else, we can capture it for study," Doc interjected.

"No." Sheriff McCoo shook his head vigorously. "No matter whether it's changed or not. I will not save the thing that killed all those people."

"Please," Alex asked. "It's those men in suits fault. My friend and I were experiments in their lab. Those guys chasing us wanted to take me back, and Dogkey was trying to protect me. That has to count for something. Aren't you supposed to help people?"

"You are people. That," He pointed at Dogkey. "Is not the case. So, I'll help you. Hop in the car, and we will go."

"My friend, too. Please. He will die if you don't help him."

"Let's just say I did the humane thing and helped it. What exactly do you expect me to do with him?"

The smell of burning flesh hung in the air as Doctor Williams and Sheriff McCoo examined Dogkey. "I think he will fit in the trunk," Doc Williams said, his voice full of sympathy. "I think the kid is right, John. You are blinded by grief. But objectively speaking, we should help the hurt animal no matter what we think of it. It could just be its nature."

McCoo sighed heavily, sending an icy chill through Alex as he opened the trunk of his squad car and grumbled, "Let's get it in the trunk. But don't ever lecture me on the difference between right and wrong again. Deal?"

Doc Williams nodded in agreement before bending down to aid Dogkey to his feet. Lifting from one side and Alex supporting him from the other, they maneuvered the heavy beast into a standing position. The trio then carefully lifted Dogkey towards the trunk but were met with resistance from their patient as he growled and showed his sharp, jagged teeth.

Alex stepped forward and looked into Dogkey's eyes. He remembered when this same animal had saved him from certain death weeks earlier and said solemnly, "They are trying to help you. Get in the trunk - it will be dark, and you will be okay. I trusted you - now trust me."

Pain etched into every inch of Dogkey's body as he finally agreed with a slow nod and allowed himself to be lowered into the makeshift refuge. The Sheriff closed the trunk lid gently before leaning against it with a long deep breath while McCoo motioned to Doc and then, to the closed lid of the squad car's trunk.

"You did the right thing," Doc Williams replied. His voice was soft and gentle, but his eyes never left the piles of smoking embers spread across the ground, remnants of small campfires that had burned out hours before.

"Those were other things from the lab," Alex said, his gaze fixed on a point beyond them. "They were part shark and part rat, I think. The men after us put them into a house, killed everyone, and waited for us to show up. We barely escaped. If it weren't for Dogkey, they would have killed me."

Sheriff McCoo stepped forward, stooping down to inspect one of the creatures still squirming beneath a pile of ash. With a swift kick, he sent the ashes flying away, exposing the tiny monster to the direct light and causing it to burst into flames, reducing it to dust within seconds. However, before it completely dissolved, its little teeth sunk into Sheriff McCoo's boot with an audible snap.

"Oww! That little thing bit clean through my boot!" He yelled in pain, hopping back as the last Shrat dissolved.

Doc Williams and Sheriff McCoo exchanged an astonished look before turning their attention back to Alex.

"You said you were from a lab," Doc questioned cautiously. "What kind of lab creates things like that?"

"I don't know, someplace out in the desert," Alex replied quietly. "They experimented on creatures and put different breeds together."

Sheriff McCoo scoffed in disbelief. "Now come on, you don't expect us to believe that? Explain those," he said, indicating the remains of the creatures scattered around them. "Explain, Dogkey. What kind of animal bursts into flames by the sun, and what kind of creature has a monkey body and a dog head? Huh? Answer me that?"

Alex stared at him wordlessly for a moment before finally replying softly: "I'm not sure. It all seems too weird."

A sudden realization then dawned on Sheriff McCoo's face as he continued: "And even if that is the case, what are you a combination of?"

"I'm different," Alex said confidently.

"What are you part 'Pain' and part 'Butt' now?" Sheriff McCoo nervously laughed and looked around the deserted back road. He ran his fingers through his greying hair and threw his arms in the air.

Doc Williams ignored the Sheriff's comment to the boy and asked, "How?"

Alex calmly told them he had died in a horse-riding accident and was brought back to life. The Sheriff laughed nervously again, throwing his hands up and pacing around his car. "Now I have heard everything! You expect us to believe that you are the walking dead?"

"Not walking dead, just brought back to life," Alex replied.

Doc Williams looked astonished, raising his eyebrows and folding his arms. "You say it like it isn't a big deal. If they have found a way to do that for people, it's nothing short of a God Blessed Miracle."

Alex scowled at the doubting Sheriff and Doctor, yelling, "It is true! Stop saying it's not!"

Doc nodded in agreement and said softly, "Either way, John, we can't let those Feds get him."

Sheriff McCoo sighed heavily and raked his fingers through his hair again. "I know that, Doc. I need time to think and a place for us to lay low. We can't go back to town."

Alex spoke up, offering a plan. "We just need to drive until dark. After that, Dogkey can protect us."

"Hold on, I'm not so sure about that," Doc interjected. "Maybe we should just hide out at Holly Weird. It's off the map, and there may be a place to secure the creature."

Sheriff McCoo said, "It's a movie set from an old western they shot on Highway 4. They built the whole town from scratch and then forgot all about it. We started calling it Holly Weird because Hollywood moviemakers do weird things like this. Get it?"

Alex nodded in understanding, unsure of what lay ahead on their journey. The three men climbed into the sheriff's car, Alex slipping into the backseat. He gazed around at the sparsely furnished interior; only a bolted mesh gate separated him from the front seat occupants.

He rested his head against the high top of the cushioned seat and could hear the soft whimpers of Dogkey in the trunk. He felt terrible for his friend but was glad that he was able to save his life. Pressing his head against the lower part of the seat, he asked, "Dogkey can you hear me?"

Dogkey grunted in response.

"If you are okay, knock on the trunk twice. If not, knock once."

Two knocks echoed from the trunk.

"Good. Do you think you will be okay?"

Two knocks echoed from the trunk.

"Good. I think we will be okay now. We are going to a deserted town to figure out what to do. The Sheriff and the Doctor seem like nice people. We should be safe from the lab there."

One knock echoed from the trunk.

"What do you mean, no? Is something wrong?"

Two knocks echoed from the trunk, signally 'Yes.'

"With the town?"

Two knocks echoed from the trunk.

"Is it safe?"

One knock echoed from the trunk.

Alex sat up and knocked on the metal fence in front of him. "We can't go to the town."

"Why?" the Sheriff asked.

"Dogkey says it's not safe. We have to go someplace else."

"I guess we're just lucky he isn't driving. Listen, kid. We're going there. That thing doesn't know what it's talking about. The town is deserted, and that's where we are headed."

CHAPTER
THIRTY-TWO

Alex woke with a sudden fear for his life. Another nightmare quickly resolved as the final moments of sleep drifted away. Using his thumb and forefinger, he stretched his tired eyes to their maximum width and looked about. The backseat of the Sheriff's car was still all around him. Rubbing the sleep from his eyes, he sat up and looked out the window. He couldn't tell for sure, but the terrain around him seemed somewhat familiar. Where had he seen it before?

"Excuse me, Sheriff," Alex said, his voice scratchy and dry. "How long have I been asleep?"

"About an hour and a half," Sheriff McCoo replied. "We should be in the town in ten minutes or so."

"Are you sure we will be safe there?"

"As safe as anywhere, I would reckon. I seriously doubt they will know to look for us there. And anyway, we are almost a hundred miles north of all that trouble you had earlier."

"North," Alex screamed. "You didn't tell me we were going north. We have to go south. Turn around."

"South, North, what's the difference?"

"That's why," Alex said, realizing why the ground outside looked familiar. He had been here before. "I think I have seen all of this before. Dogkey was right. This is dangerous."

"Just calm down, son," Doctor Williams said from the front passenger seat. "You have been through a lot. It's okay to trust someone."

"I am trusting someone, and he's in the trunk." The remaining drive into Holly Weird was filled with nothing but silence.

The Sheriff turned his car up a narrow dirt road that traveled around the far sides of the rocks. Hidden between two large rock formations, the old dirty brown buildings of the small Hollywood-built town remained hidden from view of the road. It was also why it had remained untouched; it wasn't easy to see it was there.   Once they circled the large stones, the deserted town revealed itself.

Two straight rows of two-story buildings, built to look like the ones of the old west, lined the street on both sides of a quiet dirt road and rolled on for the length of three football fields stacked end to end. At the far side of the town, more rock formations stood strategically positioned to hide the city from the view of the road. The Sheriff stopped his car in front of the tenth building on the left and stepped out.

Alex opened his door and rose to stand next to the Sheriff. The blazing sun above was blinding, and the young boy had to shield his eyes to look at the faded sign hanging on the front of the structure in front of them. "What's a Saloon?" Alex asked, reading the sign.

"It's sort of a bar," Sheriff McCoo replied. "It was a place where people gathered to talk and hang out. Come on, let's go in and sit down."

"But, what about," Alex said, motioning to the trunk. "We can't just leave Dogkey in there."

"According to you, if I open that hood, he will burst into flames," Sheriff McCoo said sarcastically. "We will wait until dark, and then I will let him out. But don't think I will take my gun off of him."

"Whatever," Alex replied, stepping onto the wooden sidewalk in front of the connected town buildings. He pushed open the four-foot-long swinging doors mounted halfway between the top of bottom of the doorframe. They squeaked loudly, giving Alex a sharp chill down his back. Ignoring the sensation, he pushed past them and entered the Saloon.

"Pretty neat, huh, kid," Doctor Williams said, looking around the Old Western replicated room.

"Yeah, sure," Albert mumbled, sitting in a chair pulled away from a table nearby. "Now, what are we going to do about the guys that are after me?"

Sheriff McCoo and Doctor Williams joined him at the table and looked as clueless as they had when they first picked him and Dogkey up. Alex lost hope and wondered if anyone could help him and his friend. He was sure they had every intention of helping them; it seemed too big a deal for them to contemplate a solution.

"I've been thinking about this," Sheriff McCoo interjected. "And I think I have a good idea."

"Let's hear it," Doc said.

"First things first, we take the boy back to his parents. The story doesn't hold much weight, but when we take him home and involve the real Feds or those not wrapped up in this whole thing, which will be more than enough proof that something is up. And then, we introduce them to Dogkey, in safe surroundings, of course. If you two become famous, these guys can't touch you."

"Hey, that's a great idea, John," Doctor Williams replied. "What do you think, kid?"

"I guess. I don't want them hurting or experimenting on Dogkey. He's a person no matter what he looks like."

"I would agree," the Doctor replied. He stood up and looked around the room. "You don't happen to remember if there is a little boy's room around here anywhere, do you."

"Sorry, "Sheriff McCoo replied. "When we drove in, I saw some dried bushes to the side of the last building we passed at the mouth of the town. Use those."

"Be right back." Doctor Williams stepped through the double squeaking doors, turned left, and disappeared around the corner of the building. "I won't forgive this indignity. But I can't hold it much longer."

"We will go back to my house at dark and switch to my car," Sheriff McCoo continued. "I have a truck with a shell, and you and your friend can travel back there together."

"Thank you," Alex reluctantly said. "You are doing the right thing. He is good. They just tortured him so much beyond just creating him. They warped him, but still, he could feel and understand. When we can let him out, I will show you and promise you that you will understand how the death of your men was not meant to happen. It is sad that they were killed, but it was how he has been treated that caused those attacks. He saw them as a threat?"

"It's going to take some mighty big selling to convince me of that, but I am willing to keep an open mind about it."

Alex smiled and smacked his palm against the table. A cloud of dust burst into the air and caused him to cough. As the dust settled, he noticed a fat beer glass with a small portion of liquid slushing across the bottom. It calmed down when the table stopped wobbling and returned to its hiding spot along the bottom of the dark rim of the glass.

"How long did you say it was since this placed was used?"

"Why?" the Sheriff asked.

"Look." Alex grabbed the glass mug by its thick handle and held it sideways to show the contents to the lawman. "Shouldn't this have evaporated or something by now."

"You're right." Sheriff McCoo stood, scooting his chair back across the floor. He looked around the room and noticed other odd things. Dust was spread across each tabletop in the room, but all the chairs were dust free. Something was not right here. "Come on. Let's go."

"Finally. You agree with me."

"No smart mouth, just stay close and follow me out. We need to go around the side and get the Doc."

CHAPTER
THIRTY-THREE

Sheriff McCoo and Alex stepped through the squeaking doors of the saloon and into the bright sun. The entire mood of the town had changed. It was still just as deserted as before, but I no longer felt safe. Instead, it felt dangerous, threatening, and, more importantly, deadly.

"Wait," Alex said. "Look."

Sheriff McCoo followed Alex's hand to the hinge of the saloon door. Someone had tightened the screws to their pressure points, causing the squeak they heard as they entered. But the most important discovery was that the screws holding the doors in place were brand new. Someone just wanted them to sound old. But why would someone do that?

"Let's go." Alex followed the Sheriff down the wooden sidewalk. They passed the general store, the bank, and even the make-believe Sheriff's office. The two people didn't pause. They continued without even looking into the passing storefront windows.

"We need to get out of here," Sheriff McCoo said, leaning around the edge of the final building, but Doctor Williams wasn't there. "Doc, where are you?"

"Where did he go?" Alex asked, joining him next to the bushes.

"I don't know. He probably just wandered off somewhere. He does that sometimes."

"Now isn't a good time. We have to leave."

"We will, kid, but not without him. Let's walk back to the saloon. Maybe he stepped into one of those stores to look around on his way back, and we didn't see him."

"If you say so," Alex replied, following the Sheriff.

Sheriff McCoo grabbed the doorknob of the first building they visited and tried to turn it but found it locked. Putting his shoulder into it, he pushed against the door, but it wouldn't budge. Convinced the Doctor wasn't in there, he brushed the dirt off his shoulder and moved on to the next building.

The second building had a substantial front store window with the words 'Dress and Pants' printed in faded red letters across the top. Alex put his face against the window to see inside while the Sheriff tried the door, but it was too dark, and he couldn't see anything. As with the one before, the entrance to this building was also locked and not budging. It was curious to Alex because the doors to an abandoned movie set were locked. It almost seemed as if someone was hiding something.

The pair came to the third door, and something in Alex instinctively told him not to let the Sheriff open it. He reached for his hand but was a second too late, and the door swung open in McCoo's left hand. Alex squinted, not knowing what to expect, but nothing happened.

"Doc, you in there?" the Sheriff called into the room. There was no response from the darkness. "If you are, speak up. We have to get out of here."

"We should just go," Alex insisted.

"I will not leave without him. That thing is your friend; he is mine, and I won't leave him behind. We should go in; he may have hurt himself and can't call out for help."

Reluctantly, Alex followed the Sheriff into the room. As they passed the doorway, he heard a slight clicking sound and looked down at the doorframe they just walked through. Positioned on the left and right of the door, tiny laser lights shined a small red beam between both battery-operated projectors. If the mysterious occupants didn't know before, whoever was hiding in this Hollywood town, now knew they were there.

"They know we are here," Alex said.

"Who?" The Sheriff asked.

"Whoever is after me."

"Would you stop? Just calm down and come on."

"Do those look safe?" Alex pointed at the lasers across the doorway. "I saw it in a movie once. When we came in, we broke that beam, which sent an alarm to someone, and I am sure they will come to check it out."

Sheriff McCoo looked into the darkness, back at the door, and back to the dark again. He wanted to see if his friend was deeper into the room but didn't want to get trapped. "Let's just check the rest of the buildings. If he doesn't answer, then I will consider leaving."

"But what about that?"

"I admit it's suspicious, but maybe the lights were used in the movie or something."

The pair left the room and continued down the boardwalk. They checked each structure, and by the time they had made it back down to the saloon, they were both tired and worried at the same time.

"It just doesn't make any sense," McCoo said, scratching his head. "Doc would have called out if something happened to him."

"Maybe they got him first."

"Who exactly are 'They'?"

"I don't know. But they want me pretty bad, and I think they will probably do anything to get Dogkey and me."

"Before we leave, let's check the stores past the saloon. I thought I saw him go the way we went, but maybe he went the other way. We will check those and then the other side, and if we don't find him, we will go for help."

"Are you sure that's smart? If you check everywhere, whoever is here will get us."

"I can protect us," Sheriff McCoo said, patting the pistol loosely riding on his right hip.

"I don't know how to drive, so I am stuck with you. But for the record, I think this is a bad idea."

Alex and the Sheriff went from building to building. Most had locked doors, but the ones they could open were empty and void of clues to the missing Doctor. Each room they looked in seemed more vacant than the one before. In addition, Alex found no other laser lights across the doorways and was beginning to think that the Sheriff had been right about it being a movie leftover. Something about the town felt wrong, and Alex wondered if it was making him more frightened than he would typically be.

Eight buildings later, Alex sat on a small wooden bench before a barbershop. He leaned over his knees and tried to catch his breath in the searing heat. "I need to rest a minute. It's scorching out here," Alex said.

"Sure," the Sheriff replied, sitting beside the boy. "Nothing has come after us since we arrived an hour ago. I am betting no one's here."

"You had to say that," Alex replied, standing up.

Sheriff McCoo followed the boy's gaze to a group of seven men across the street. They stepped out of a small building in the line of connected structures, across the wooden sidewalk, and into the dirty lane. As they stepped into the bright light of the road, the Sheriff instantly recognized them as more of the same type of Federal Agents he had met before.

"Run," the Sheriff whispered as he stepped into the street. He waved his hand to the approaching Agents and smiled as big as he could. "Hey boys, glad to see you. I think we found what you are looking for."

From the corner of his eye, the Sheriff could see that Alex hadn't run yet. Why wouldn't that boy listen to him? He turned his head slightly to the side and whispered, "Do what I told you?"

"I couldn't hear you," Alex responded. "What did you say?"

The Agents grew closer. The Sheriff could see the blue-suited feds clearer now and was not surprised to see that each man carried an automatic weapon in their right hand. Against the six-shot pistol he carried to his side, he knew he wouldn't be a match for them. But maybe he could buy the boy some time to get away.

"Run," Sheriff McCoo whispered again. He didn't want the Agents to hear him.

"Huh," Alex replied.

"Run!" the Sheriff yelled, frustrated. He pushed the boy toward the direction of the car and drew his weapon. Waiting until the boy was several feet away, Sheriff McCoo bolted after him.

The Agents each raised their weapons and squeezed their triggers. A storm of bullets shot out toward the Sheriff and Alex. Alex was far enough ahead that the men couldn't simultaneously shoot at him and the Sheriff. They concentrated their fire on the lawman.

Sheriff McCoo thought he would make it to safety. As he passed a ceramic horse and through two buildings down from the saloon, he felt an incredible pain in his shoulder and left leg. A burning sensation followed the pain, and he instantly recognized the feeling. He had been shot a few times. He had fired his gun behind him, knocking an Agent down with each bullet, but they had him outgunned, and it was only a matter of time before they caught him.

The bullets sent the Sheriff stumbling forward as more pierced his body. As he fell, he saw Alex dart into the saloon to avoid a barrage of incoming bullets. The boy was safe for now, but unless there was a back door, he was sure that the kid would also share his fate.

The pain from the bullet wounds was incredible. His whole body throbbed, and Sheriff McCoo found it hard to move. He lay on his stomach, wiggling in pain as he heard the soft approach of the Agents behind him. They stopped beside him, grabbed him by both shoulders, and flipped him over to his back. He wiped away the dirt in his eyes and looked up at the Agents.

"Hello, John," Doctor Williams said.

"Doc, they got you too," Sheriff McCoo replied, staring at his old friend. "I'm sorry."

"Not exactly. I'm sorry it had to come to this, but you have just gotten too close. Why couldn't you listen to me? I tried to steer you away, but you wouldn't do it. You had to be the hero."

"I don't understand. You fought with them at the diner, you..." The Sheriff trailed off, coming to grips with his friend betraying him. It didn't seem possible, but here he was.

"I couldn't pass up the opportunity," Doctor Williams explained. "We made creatures beyond imagination and crossed the boundaries of life and death. When would I ever get that opportunity again? I had to go to work for them. It was everything I got into science for."

"But all your talk of what's wrong and right. Was that just a lie? You have to know that this isn't right. That poor boy is being terrorized."

"That poor boy is dead. We brought him back to life. That makes him ours. As far as what's wrong or right, you can be gullible sometimes. And I am a pretty good actor, hmmm."

"I have met your wife. We had dinner together at your house. Was all of that an act?"

"Not all of it. Clara doesn't know what I am doing. But other than that, yeah, all an act."

"What are you going to do with me?"

"Now, that is a dilemma, isn't it," Doc replied. He turned back to the Agents. "Go get the boy and bring him back to me. I will deal with the Sheriff here. And the General has expressed his strong desire for you to catch him alive, please. We don't want to try the re-animate process so soon."

"Yes, sir," the Agents replied. They ran towards the still-swinging doors of the saloon.

"You didn't answer my question." Sheriff McCoo spit a mouthful of blood on the shoes of his former friend.

"I have to kill you, John. I don't have any choice."

CHAPTER
THIRTY-FOUR

Alex could hear the bullets splintering the wood near his heels. He knew that it was only a matter of seconds before they hit him. A few feet before him, he saw the swinging doors of the Saloon blowing back and forth in the wind. He wasn't sure if he could make it, but he dove towards them anyway. Pleasantly surprised, he slid through the doorway, escaping the last storm of gunfire.

Rising to a crouch, Alex peeked out the corner of the building's front window. Four of the blue-coated Agents were slowly walking toward his position. Each was taking the time to reload the weapons they held tightly in their hands. Turning away from the window, he looked through the abandoned movie set for a safe hiding place. But where?

He thought about running up the stairs but was afraid he would be trapped, and they would surround him. He had been in that situation before and was lucky last time. He didn't think he could escape twice. His only chance was to hide somewhere on the first floor, let them pass by him, and then run out the door when they weren't looking. It was simple. He told himself it was a good solid plan. But where was he going to hide?

Alex looked behind the bar and opened a few doors to some closets, but everything looked obvious. They would think to look there. Then he saw it, the perfect hiding place. A sizeable old-fashioned piano was across the room, pushed up against a wall in the corner. The lid was propped open halfway with a wooden stick keeping it at a forty-five-degree angle to the rest of the piano. They would never think to look for him there.

Alex ran across the room and climbed into the inner workings of the large black piano. He gently laid across the large wire strings and raised his legs to brace the piano lid with his feet. He removed the stick holding up the piano lid and immediately felt its weight against his legs. Slowly bending his legs, he softly lowered the lid shut. The space was tighter than Alex had initially thought, but he felt safe and was happy that a small crack existed between the piano and its lid. He could see the whole saloon from his hiding spot.

The four Agents entered the room and immediately spread throughout the room. As expected, they turned over tables, opened closets, and looked behind the bar. The piano was the only place they didn't think to look. Frustrated, they regrouped at the base of the stairs and whispered something to each other. Seconds later, they started up the stairs to the second floor. Alex watched them disappear up the staircase and took a deep breath.

Alex counted to ten and pushed the lid open with his feet. He opened it to its previous height and reached over to prop it open with the stick, but he couldn't find the piece of wood. Looking to his left and right, he frantically searched for the wood but couldn't see it.

His legs were getting tired, and Alex knew the Agents would be coming down soon. He had to find a way out of here. Starring at his feet, an idea came to him. Slowly, he lowered the lid again and hastily removed both oversized shoes from his feet. He pushed the top back up with his bare feet and wedged his shoes between the lid and the piano. Carefully, he lowered the lid again and released his feet as the cover rested against the boots. He carefully watched the shoes, making sure they wouldn't give out.

The gap between the lid and the piano was small, but he thought he could fit through it. Going first, Alex slipped his feet, legs, and waist through the gap. As he prepared to squeeze out his torso and head, he saw the shoes start to shake; they were bending. The gap began to shrink, and he didn't think he could get his upper body through without pushing on the lid, but if he did this, he would have to let it slam, and then the Agents upstairs would hear it and come running. But he didn't have any other choice. He pushed on the lid and slid out. The shoes bent in on each other and fell away from the gap. The top came crashing down against the piano, splintering the old wood. A loud crash echoed through the Saloon.

"Oh, no," Alex mumbled, pausing where he stood. He could hear the Agents running back towards the stairs.

Sheriff McCoo looked up at his one-time friend in shock. He couldn't believe the man he had trusted for so many years was not only betraying him but was going to kill him. How could he have been so fooled? As a Sheriff, he should be able to see the bad guys around him, not befriend them.

"Goodbye, John," Doc Williams said, leveling the gun on the lawman's head. "For what it's worth, I liked you."

The Doctor wrapped his finger around the trigger and felt the cold metal against his skin. He took a deep breath and pulled the trigger. A loud crash echoed out of the saloon as he squeezed his index finger. It sounded as if the whole second floor had crashed in. Surprised, Doc's hand jerked slightly to the left at the sound of the crash, and he misfired into the dirt next to Sheriff McCoo.

McCoo wasn't going to give up the opportunity. The Doctor looked to the saloon's swinging doors, not realizing he had missed the Sheriff. He lost control of the gun in his right hand, and it spun away. He swung out at the Doctor with his good leg and swept his feet from beneath him. Before he realized what was happening, Doctor Williams tumbled uncontrollably backward.

Hitting the ground hard, Doc gasped in pain as the air rushed out of his lungs. The back of his head collided with a four-inch round rock on the ground, dazing him as he fought to catch his breath. The Sheriff didn't want to give the Doctor a chance to recover. He tried to stand, but with the bullet wound in his leg, he found he couldn't. The bullet in his leg and shoulder was making it too painful. Instead of walking, he scooted over to the Doctor, pulling and pushing himself with his good limbs. As he approached Doctor Williams, he saw the man was beginning to regain his breath. He didn't wait for the Doctor to recover fully before he struck him in the face. The Sheriff's fist collided with the traitor's forehead twice before his former friend's eyes rolled back in his head. The Doctor fought hard to keep his consciousness but, unfortunately, found it too difficult and passed out.

Although it was difficult with his injuries, the Sheriff managed to roll Doc over on his stomach and handcuff his hands behind his back. He didn't want his friend sneaking up behind him. Once his attacker was safely secured, he scrambled in the dirt for his gun and began scooting toward the saloon.

CHAPTER
THIRTY-FIVE

Alex hadn't expected the crash to be so loud, but the piano lid echoed. Not waiting to collect his shoes, he quickly ran for the door barefoot. He had made it barely outside the swinging doors when he heard the rushing steps of the Agents coming down the stairs behind him.

"Stop right there, kid and raise your hands," one of the similar-looking Agents said. "We would rather take you alive, but if there is no other way, we will shoot you. They can always bring you back."

Alex didn't know what else he could do. He raised his hands and rotated to face the Agents. Smiling, the Agents lowered their weapons and walked toward the small boy. Alex backed up until he bumped into the front of the Sheriff's car and then stopped to await the Agents. He looked to his left and right but had nowhere to escape. He was trapped.

"Glad that you see it our way," one of the blue-suited Agents said, pushing open the swinging doors.

GROWL!

The Agents froze. They raised their weapons and quickly looked around the surrounding area. Suddenly, the lid to the Sheriff's trunk burst into the air. It flew several feet and landed in the dirt. Dogkey stood up in the back of the squad car, growled loudly, and leaped towards the Agents. The sun immediately started to burn the monster, and by the time he reached the Blue suited men, they saw a ferocious cloud of smoke. The large form of the half dog, half monkey barreled over Alex's head. He ducked with a smile and cheered on his friend.

Dogkey fought through the pain and collided with the Agents. All of them rolled into the Saloon. The light from the window continued to burn the creature, but he found it not as bad as direct sunlight and began to fight with gentle care. As he hurt the blue-suited men, he moved around, trying to stay in the minimized shadows.

Alex rushed in after his friend and could see the monster fighting the Agents, but he was not using his claws or teeth. Dogkey wasn't trying to kill them, just incapacitate the attackers. Alex smiled. He got through to his friend. The creature was no longer killing. However, in the case of the agents, he wouldn't have minded lots of pain, cuts, and broken bones.

One of the four blue-suited Agents fired his weapon at Dogkey's giant form, but the bullet missed wide to the right. The animal swung its huge paw and slid the smoking gun across the floor. He picked up the man and threw him across the room. The Fed hit the wall several feet from the floor and slid down to the ground. The Agent tried to stand but lost consciousness and fell back to the earth.

The second blue-dressed man fired at the hairy beast, and the bullet penetrated Dogkey's hip. No blood spilled. It seemed to ricochet off the bone and disappear into the wood panel beside him. The creature didn't wait for him to fire a second time. He reached out, grabbed the weapon, and broke it in half. Metal scraps flew into the agent's face. The man screamed in pain and ran out of the saloon covering the bleeding wounds on his face. As he passed Alex, the boy stuck out his foot and tripped the frightened bad guy.

The third and fourth Agents were back on their feet. They recovered their automatic weapons and fired at the smoking creature, but Dogkey was too quick. He jumped left, then right, then up, and then down. They suffered the brunt of the creature's first attack.

Unbeknownst to the attackers, Dogkey made his way closer to them with each dodging movement. Within a few moments, he was on top of them. Grabbing them both by their necks, he lifted the identical men in the air and banged their heads together. After the first collision, the men seemed drugged and dizzy. The creature swung their heads together a second time and dropped them when he saw them drift un-conscious. Their bodies were crippled as they hit the ground.

The burning from the sun was starting to hurt Dogkey deeply, and Alex knew it. He rushed in as his friend dropped the last two Agents. "Hurry," Alex said. "Let's get in you into the closet."

Alex rushed Dogkey across the floor and into a closet next to the staircase. He shoved his friend in, stepped in behind him, and closed the door. The small room was filled with the scent of burning flesh and the smoke coming off the creature's skin. Alex wondered how his friend could handle it.

"Thank you very much," Alex said, patting his friend on the shoulder. "You saved me again."

Dogkey patted him back and gently hugged him. He knew the creature was saying you're welcome.

"I noticed," Alex continued. "You didn't kill any of those men. I am proud of you." Alex could feel his friend smile. "I need to go see if anyone else is coming. You wait here, and I will be back."

Dogkey grabbed Alex by the shoulder and wouldn't let go.

"I have to go," Alex said. "I need to check on the Sheriff and make sure no one is still out there. I'll be right back."

The creature reluctantly released Alex. The boy stepped out of the closet and shut the door behind him. Dogkey sat silently in the dark, trying to listen as he did in the car's trunk for any danger to the boy. He heard his friend go outside, then nothing but silence. Waiting, as Alex had asked, the creature remained quiet. He hoped Alex was all right.

A few minutes passed, and Alex didn't return. Dogkey waited several more minutes, and when he was confident that Alex wouldn't return, the creature decided to step back into the sun. He knew it would hurt, but he couldn't let anything happen to his friend.

Dogkey pushed open the door and stepped out. The first floor of the Saloon area was empty. The creature hated to do it, but he stepped up to the swinging doors and returned to the sunlight.

"No, Dogkey. It's a trap," Alex yelled, wiggling from the arms of the two men holding him.

The creature turned towards Alex's screaming and had a split second to see him being held by two blue-suited Agents and surrounded by ten more. The men holding his friend didn't give him time to react. A man with a flamethrower strapped tightly to his back stepped forward, raised the barrel, and fired toward the smoking creature.

He tried to twist away, but the flame covered too much of an area, engulfing him in a blaze of fire. The pain was too much for the creature, his legs went limp, and he dropped to the ground. He couldn't fight the sensations running through his body. The monster went limp and couldn't resist the agony any longer. He waited for the end, hoping his pain would fade with death.

Alex dropped to his knees and cried. The Agents grabbed him and dragged him off. The man with a flamethrower was satisfied that the monster would not be getting back up. He turned and followed Alex and the rest of the Agents down the wooden sidewalk. They entered the building where Alex had noticed the earlier red light across the doorway.

The Agents and Alex filed into the room and shut the door behind them. He looked around, wondering what they were going to do. He soon got his answer as the entire floor lowered to the ground. Alex hadn't caught it before, but the building was a large elevator. Sinking deeper into the Earth, he found himself not even thinking of his situation. He was sad about his friend and wanted to make these men pay.

Sheriff McCoo crawled closer to the saloon. The pain was making it hard for him to move. He had helplessly watched the Agents take Alex and disappear into a building near the end of the street, but not before they lit the monster on fire. He had no reason to save the beast but watched as it tried to protect Alex and wondered if he had been wrong. If nothing else, he did owe the Monster for distracting his old friend, Doc, and allowing him to escape.

Pulling himself as quickly as his body would allow, the Sheriff made his way to the screaming pile of smoke that was Dogkey. He removed his shirt and patted out the fires burning across the creature's body. Patches of fir were gone entirely and revealed burnt-red skin below. Putting out the flames was only part of the problem. The sun was still up, and the monster's sensitive skin was smoking from the golden rays blanketing the town. The soft whimpering of the animal made the lawman feel for him. He had been wrong. But what was he going to do about it? He wasn't strong enough to take him in the shadows.

Dogkey rolled his head over to the Sheriff and made eye contact. The soft red eyes were filled with pain and fear. It was helpless to save itself but somehow wanted to communicate the need to be out of the sun.

The Sheriff already knew this. Awkwardly, he patted the suffering animal on the shoulder and said, "It will be all right. I will think of something." And as promised, he did.

Placing his good shoulder against Dogkey, Sheriff McCoo pushed with all his might and rolled the creature into the street. His body dropped from the wood and rolled twice until it stopped several feet from the Sheriff's vehicle. A look of bewilderment spread across the monster's face, but he didn't fight the lawman. The man was trying to help him.

McCoo painfully crawled into the street, scooted up against the creature again, and pushed a second time. Dogkey slowly rolled forward, and it wasn't until they had made it close to the Sheriff's car that the creature understood what was happening. He tried to move his body to help the hurt human. Several more attempts later, the Sheriff rolled Dogkey to the squad car's underside. Once there, Dogkey slipped under the vehicle and out of the sun.

"There you go," Sheriff McCoo said, dropping into the dirt. He tried to move his body, but it hurt too badly. Soon he lost consciousness and didn't expect ever to wake again.

CHAPTER THIRTY-SIX

Alex woke in total darkness. He wasn't sure how long he had been asleep, but he knew exactly where he was. It was the place of his dreams. Or, more accurately, his nightmares. He was back in the pitch-black holding cells of the Lab. Instinctively, he looked up, hoping to meet the glowing red eyes of Dogkey, but then remembered his friend wasn't alive anymore. He was left to burn in the blazing sun.

The thought of his dead friend angered the young boy and sent him running to the room's only door. It was easy to find, with the tiny slit at the bottom of the doorjamb being the only light source. Alex moved his hands back and brought them forward with all his strength against the door.

"Let me out," Alex yelled, beating on the door repeatedly. Every ounce of anger in him flowed through his hands, and the metal door felt the ferocity of his inner pain. He knew he had no chance of breaking through the steel. It had been made to subdue Dogkey. But it did make him feel a lot better to hit it. "You can't keep me here. I have rights."

"Step away from the door," a deep voice ordered through a speaker mounted somewhere in the darkness.

"I won't," Alex replied.

"Move back," the voice commanded. "Or this conversation will become very uncomfortable for you."

Alex continued to pound on the door for several more minutes but stopped when he heard a crucial turn in the lock, and the bolt on the door clicked. He stepped back and watched as it swung open slowly. With his eyes adjusted for the darkness, the harsh light from the doorway was blinding, forcing him to cover his eyes until they could acclimate.

Slowly moving his arms away, Alex fluttered his eyes until he could see the silhouette of a man in the doorway. The shadow turned into a featureless person, and then the features began to fade into view. It was the man from the dream, the scar-faced General.

"Your time away from us has seemed to rile you up," the General said, smiling in a sinister manner.

"I don't belong here. Why won't you let me go?"

"I can't think of any place you belong more than here. You are ours. We own you."

"You don't own me. I have rights."

"No, you don't," the General said, laughing between each word. "You have no doubt found out by now that you are a little subject of ours, a successful experiment, I might add. But what you may not have discovered is that you died. We brought you back."

"I know that," Alex replied.

"Really? I must say that I am impressed. Nevertheless, after you died, your rights died with you. Technically you are a walking corpse, and the last time I checked the Constitution, corpses don't have any rights."

"I was dead, but I am alive now. That means that...."

"It means nothing," the General interrupted. "All that matters is that we have you, and you are ours. Now I would appreciate it if you would stay quiet. It's hard to think about our other projects while you are making such a racket."

"What are you going to do with me?"

"Not that it matters, but we will continue experimenting on you. Do you know we have injected you with seven diseases, including cancer, palsy, and Aids?"

"You didn't?"

"Yes, we did. And since bringing you back, your body has fought each illness successfully. All of those I named and some that I can't have passed through you and left you healthy."

"Why?"

"The research is incredible, and the material is very vital. Through your cooperation, we will be able to accomplish so much more. This is one reason I am glad to have you back."

"I don't care what you say or what you want. I won't do anything for you. You killed my friend."

"Your friend? Do you mean that monkey thing I had my men put down? That was barely an animal."

"Regardless of your thoughts, you didn't have to kill him. If I'm so important to you, why didn't you bring him down alive too? Dogkey was an extraordinary and fantastic being."

"That is up to interpretation. I, for one, found him tiresome and annoying. But that was not why we didn't bring him down with you. It was much simpler than that. He killed a human, several actually," the General said, nodding his head. "Once they taste the man in their mouth, it's all over. Besides, don't worry. We liked that creation. We're already planning on another one. But instead of putting it with you, we put it in the cage with the half Elephant, a half-lion creature. If they survive each other, it will be quite interesting."

"You're the monster, not them. You keep us against our will, experiment, and God knows what else. The police will find you. There is no way that you will get away with this."

"Such a naïve little boy. We own the police. As a federal agency, they report to us in these cases. I guess you could say that makes us the police. And I highly doubt that we will find what we do offensive to ourselves. Good day and I do see that you quit the racket. I would hate to drop a few of the shrats in here with you. They can be very nasty, but I think you know that."

The General exited the room and shut the door behind him. Alex was thrust back into the darkness. He sat on the floor and stared at the light from beneath the door. He had to find a way out, but how. Tears formed in the corner of his eyes. He tried to hold them back but found he couldn't. Lowering his head into his hands, he began to cry uncontrollably.

CHAPTER THIRTY-SEVEN

Sheriff John McCoo slowly regained consciousness and was genuinely surprised to be alive. He had expected his next destination to be beyond this world and was somewhat disappointed. The area around him looked different. There was no street, no town, just the four small walls of the room surrounding the small twin bed he was lying in.

Sitting up, he saw that his wounds had been wrapped in bandages. It wasn't the prettiest first aid wrappings he had seen, but it appeared to have done the trick. He peeled back the gauze on his leg and shoulder, happy the bullets had passed through him. This and the fact that someone had applied enough pressure to stop the bleeding had saved his life.

In the corner of the room, Dogkey rose and approached the bed. The tall form of the mighty creature towered over the recovering Sheriff and was somewhat intimidating to the lawman.

"Did you do this for me?" Sheriff McCoo asked, speaking slowly, and wondering if the monster could understand him.

Dogkey nodded in agreement and attempted a smile. The corners of the monster's large dog snout mouth could barely rise a centimeter, but it was enough to help McCoo understand.

"Thank you. You saved my life."

Dogkey looked around the room. Sheriff McCoo couldn't tell what he wanted, but the creature seemed frantically needing something. The monster locked its eyes on a dirty old chair on its side in the corner. He picked it up, brought it over to the bedside of the Sheriff, and began to scribble in the dust covering its seat. With extreme interest, McCoo watched the words form, smiled when Dogkey finished, and held it up for the lawman.

"Welcome. You save me, I save you," the Sheriff read out loud, surprised the sentence was understandable. "Where did Alex go?"

"I know what building they took him into, but I am not sure what happened to him after that." Sheriff McCoo made eye contact with Dogkey and shook his head.

Dogkey began to write again. When finished, he held it back up for Sheriff McCoo to read.

"It dark soon. I will go get him," the Sheriff read again and turned his attention to the creature. "Let's go get him together." He crawled out of bed, and although his injured leg was a little shaky, he found he could stand.

Dogkey handed the Sheriff his shirt back. As he put it on, he smiled at the various holes and burn marks spread across it. The ragged old shirt barely had enough material to hold itself together, but he put it on anyway. The badge still showed, and he wanted these guys to know who was coming to take the boy back.

Sheriff McCoo led Dogkey out of the room. They found themselves on the second floor of the Saloon. With a great deal of care, he slowly made it down the stairs. Dogkey, recovering from burns across most of his hairy body, followed behind at the same pace. He wasn't sure how long he had been out, but it was dark out, and he knew this would be their time to get the kid back.

"What a pair we are with both of our injuries," Sheriff McCoo said with a smile. "I have a few things in the trunk of my car that might help us get the kid back if you didn't crush them while you were back there. If nothing else, we might be able to even the odds in our favor slightly."

CHAPTER
THIRTY-EIGHT

Alex sat quietly in total darkness. He wondered if this, too, was an experiment. Maybe they were trying to see how long a kid could live alone in a locked room. It had been several hours since he was ordered to stop pounding, and since then, no one had come to see him, not even to bring food. He was starving but refused to ask his captors for anything.

As if somebody had been reading his mind, the door to the black room opened, and two men rushed in and grabbed him by each arm. They dragged him from the room by force, and Alex found himself in a familiar laboratory. The place they had completed tests on him, the place they had hurt him. His forgotten memory of the horrors done to him suddenly rushed back on him. In his mind's eye, he could see each experiment and feel the pain and agony he had experienced each time. It was mind-numbing, and his legs gave out. He was tired of being forced and dragged. This was the worst place they could have taken him.

"What are you going to do with me?" Alex asked. His energy was low, and try as he could, the boy could barely raise his voice.

The two men in white lab coats didn't answer. They lifted him onto an icy steel table. They strapped his arms to the side of the sterile surface and then secured his feet. When completed, they disappeared from his view. He turned to look around but found the lab was mostly empty. A few people lingered before miscellaneous computers and test tubes, but nothing as he had dreamed.

"Good evening, Chromosome 19," the General said, scratching the scar on his face as he smiled. "I do appreciate you stopping that insidious pounding on the door. I take it you had a good rest."

"No," Alex replied. "I want to go home."

"I think we have already discussed that item, and I believe you know my response."

"What more do you want to do? Haven't you tested enough?"

"It's late in the evening, and many of our staff have gone home, but one can never do too much testing. I don't expect someone as young as yourself to understand this, but we have only begun to scratch the surface. We will block some of your arteries with high fat and cholesterol tonight. It should be most interesting. I hope the somatic cell manipulation is as kind to you tonight as it has been in the past."

"Why would you keep doing this?"

"Isn't it obvious by now because we can? And because we are curious to see what will happen."

"You think that Dogkey is a monster. He is nothing compared to you and the people helping with this."

"Sticks and stones will break my bones, but names will never hurt me. Give me a break, kid."

"And now you are going to turn me into a monster with that somatic cell stuff you said. What will happen? Will I grow horns?"

A nurse appeared from nowhere and fitted a mask across his face. Gas-filled the plastic mouth cover, and Alex felt very sleepy. Although the gas had no odor he could identify, it left a very metallic taste in his mouth. He tried to keep his eyes open but could not fight the urge to close them. Drifting to sleep, the last thing Alex saw was the smiling face of the General.

The General leaned over Alex and mouthed, "No monster for you tonight, just your arteries and blood. We need to see if you can live through anything. And again, why do we do this? Because we can, kid, and you can't do anything about it."

Sheriff McCoo and Dogkey made their way to the back of the Sheriff's car. As expected, some of his items had been crushed by the massive weight of the monster. But to the Sheriff's happiness, the most important things were still intact and looked to be in functioning order.

"This will help even the odds," Sheriff McCoo commented as he pulled out an M-16 semi-automatic rifle and slapped a magazine of bullets into the open slot below the barrel. Next, he picked up six hand grenades and stuffed two in each of his front pockets and one in each of his back pockets.

"These are grenades. I pull this metal pin out, throw it, and a few seconds later, it explodes."

Dogkey shook his head in acknowledgment.

"I know what you're thinking," the Sheriff said, looking at the odd expression on Dogkey's face. "Why does a small-town Sheriff have all of these weapons? We had a problem with some biker gangs a few years ago. They caught us with our pants down, and several of my deputies were hurt. One died. After that, I had each car stored with a few extra pieces of equipment. Can you fire a weapon?"

Dogkey shook his head no.

"That's okay. I think you are dangerous just the way you are." Sheriff McCoo reached up to close the lid of the trunk and realized it wasn't there. He remembered that Dogkey had pulled it from its hinges and thrown it several yards away. Looking up at the monster, McCoo feigned an expression of anger. A moment later, he smiled, and they started on their way to the building that Alex had been taken to. "Did you have to rip the lid off the hinges?"

Dogkey shrugged.

The Agents had disappeared. Stopping outside the door, McCoo remembered this was the only room with a red light mounted near the door. It was some signal to the people in the lab or the duplicate Agents. He had dismissed it earlier but now believed the boy had been right about it.

Dogkey moved to open the door, but the Sheriff pushed his hand against the hairy creature's chest and stopped him. "There is an alert on the door. If we go that way, they will know we are here. Let's try this way."

McCoo took a step over to the front window of the building and attempted to open the window. After fiddling with it for a few moments, he gave up, stepped back, and smashed it out with the butt of his rifle. It shattered completely, leaving only small fragments in the corners. He cleared the glass from the edges of the frame and climbed in. Once in the building, he froze and watched the area as Dogkey followed through the window.

"Wait here," McCoo whispered. He opened every door on the first floor and was disappointed when he found no passageways leading into hidden areas. Based on the lab the boy had described, it would have to be a big area with lots of space for storage rooms. "Where could they have gone?"

Dogkey motioned for him to come to him. McCoo was halfway across the room to Dogkey when the creature held up his hand, motioning for him to stop. Bewildered, McCoo stopped and stared at the beast. The hairy mix breed pulled down on a hook mounted to the wall's wood next to the door, and the room began to shake. Slowly, it lowered into the ground.

"How did you know?" Sheriff McCoo asked, perplexed by the complexity of the monster's solution. It was odd enough that the entire first floor was an elevator, but the fact that the creature knew was even more bizarre.

The floor that continued to lower them was layered with dust and grime. The creature bent over and scribbled a few words in the dirt to answer the Sheriff's question. After Dogkey finished writing, he read it once to himself, stood up, and pointed for McCoo to read.

"This is the way I escaped. I have been here before," the Sheriff read. McCoo was embarrassed and nodded to the creature. "I guess so."

The two of them continued to lower more profoundly into the ground. Looking up, McCoo figured they had traveled at least twenty stories straight down. The air was getting cooler, indicating they were entering a conditioned environment. The elevator floor started to slow down, and the Sheriff raised his weapon. He could tell they were moments from the bottom.

The floor came to a stop about thirty stories from the ground level. A soft click echoed through the room, and one entire wall slid open like a door. The corridor outside was quiet and void of any people. Sheriff McCoo had expected a welcoming party to meet them and try to capture them as soon as they arrived but was surprised to find no one there.

"Where do you think they all are?" McCoo asked the friendly creature hovering behind him. Dogkey lowered to write into the ground but stopped when McCoo touched his right shoulder. "Oh, never mind, I keep forgetting you can't talk. Just forget it."

McCoo led them out of the odd elevator and into several battleship gray hallways. Doors with numbers lined the halls on each side about every ten feet. His first thoughts were of the holding cells the kid had described. He wondered if there was a creature or child behind each locked door. But he couldn't focus on that. He had to get the boy and bring these guys down. If he were successful, there would be time enough later to free everyone or everything else.

Halfway down the sterile hallway, McCoo stopped when he noticed Dogkey drop down on all fours and start sniffing the air. "Do you smell him?"

Dogkey shook his head up and down. Suddenly, the echo of screaming filtered down the hall. Both the Sheriff and the monster recognized it. The voice belonged to Alex, who sounded in considerable pain. Quickly, they rushed down the corridor.

CHAPTER
THIRTY-NINE

"I can't feel my arms or legs," Alex screamed at the top of his lungs. "What have you done to me?"

The General leaned over the boy and smiled. The raised corners of his mouth staggered the scar and made the evil man look even more scary than before. "You're feeling will return to your limbs soon enough. Unfortunately, we could not do it for your mouth, but they tell me it's too close to your brain and could do some permanent damage. But it would have been grand to experience the silence. Perhaps we will knock you out again with gas."

"Let me go."

"At this point, why would it matter? You can't move your body. Where would you go?"

"With us," Sheriff McCoo said, clicking off the safety of the M-16. A soft click echoed through the large lab. Most of the technicians weren't sure what the sound was, but after years of military service, the General knew instantly the sound of someone removing the safety and arming their weapon.

"Oh, you must be the illusive Sheriff John McCoo," the General said, spinning around to view the voice behind him. Surprised, the commanding officer took a double take when he saw the large form of the escaped monster slightly behind the lawman's left shoulder. "And you brought a friend, I see. Doctor Williams did say you were resourceful. I guess he was right."

"You are all under arrest," the Sheriff ordered, waving his gun from side to side. "Put your hands on your head and get down on your knees."

From all around McCoo, individuals burst into laughter. He wasn't sure what was so funny about his statement. Scanning the people, he could detect no fear or concern on their faces. They appeared to know something he didn't, but what was it, and how bad was it for him?

"I mean it." Sheriff McCoo motioned the weapon in his hands to the general. "I have no problem with using force."

"I'm sure you don't," commented the General. "But as you will see, neither do I."

Dogkey tapped McCoo on the shoulder. The Sheriff turned and could see the halls filled with blue-suited duplicate Agents. They held a handgun pointed directly at them in each of their hands.

"So that's how you want to play it?" Sheriff McCoo said.

"Exactly. I like to think we are quite secure in our little facility here. You should know better than to think we would have one little red light protecting this location. We have hidden cameras and invisible sensors. And you have met my agents. Aren't they just wondrous?"

"They're freaks. They all look alike. Where are the test tubes?"

"Not the first one. But yes, I tubed the rest once I created the first one and got all of the adeno-associated virus vectors correctly integrated into the chromosome. I figured why, re-create when you can duplicate. Wouldn't you?"

Sheriff McCoo didn't acknowledge the General. Instead, he looked around the room and thought about possible escape plans.

"You really should reply when people talk to you. It's the polite thing to do," the General said. "But if you had thought about the security here, we wouldn't have to have this conversation. So, I guess either way, it's your fault."

"I will occupy their attention. Get the boy," McCoo whispered to Dogkey. He turned back to the General and returned the fake smile. "It wasn't that I didn't think about it. I didn't care. NOW!" McCoo pulled a grenade from his pocket, pulled the pin loosely from the top, and rolled it down the hall into the cluster of Agents. He knew he only had a few seconds before it would explode and leaped forward behind a table.

Dogkey had already begun to move. He leaped the length of the entire room and was at Alex's side when the explosion erupted. The bright blast shook the facility as air and flame burst through the hall. The General and his technicians near the grenade flew across the room from the pressure, but not Dogkey. His strong legs held him in place until the blast subsided.

"You're alive," Alex exclaimed, tears forming. "I thought they killed you."

Dogkey tore at the straps and freed his friend. He backed away from the table to see if there was any danger and was surprised to see no one coming for them. He turned back to Alex and motioned for him to follow.

"I can't move," Alex said, wiggling his nose. "Just my face, nothing else. You'll have to carry me."

Dogkey gently picked Alex up and looked for the shortest route of escape.

Most of the Agents in the first hallway were not moving, and those who could, wiggled in pain and agony from the grenade fragments. The two remaining hallways leading into the lab filled with Agents, and McCoo wasted no time firing his rifle toward them. Bullets riddled the walls of the hall. Some connected with Agents, knocking them to the floor, while other shots forced the men back the way they came. Dogkey huddled down behind the Sheriff and showed him he had rescued Alex from the table.

"How are you doing, kid?" the Sheriff asked.

"I can't move, and they shot my body full of fat and cholesterol. But other than that, I'm fine," Alex sarcastically responded.

"Hey, when this is over, maybe I can give you some of mine. The Doc tells me I have too much of both. If you can believe what he says. But first, we have to get out of here. Any ideas?"

"You didn't come in with a plan?"

"Don't judge. We got you, didn't we? I just figured it would be easier to get out of here."

The two hallways filled with Agents again. They seemed more determined to capture or kill the three outsiders. Firing their weapons, they began to move toward the lab. They stepped over their fallen comrades with no regard for their motionless corpses. McCoo reached into his pocket and pulled out another grenade.

"I would duck if I were you." McCoo pulled the pin from the pear-shaped weapon and tossed it into the closest hallway. As before, the grenade exploded with a force to rock the room. The after result was different this time. Dust and rock sprayed down across the lab from the roof above. The clean lab was now covered in a thick layer of dirt.

"I think the explosions are loosening the ceiling. We need to get out of here before the whole roof caves in," McCoo said, standing up and firing his gun at the approaching Agents.

"There are other victims down here. We can't just leave them. It wouldn't be right," Alex exclaimed.

"I am more concerned with staying alive," Sheriff McCoo said, throwing a third grenade down the last hallway. "But we will free as many as we can. Do you know if all of these cells are full?"

A piece of the ceiling formed a crack and came loose. It spiraled down from above, crushing two unconscious technicians below it. More dirt and rock sprayed through the newly created hole.

In the far corner of the room, the General began to stir. He recovered from the force of the grenade blast as he was sprayed with tiny particles of rock. He opened his eyes and was furious at the damage done to his laboratory. Someone was going to pay for it. He could see the Sheriff and that infuriating monster hiding behind a barrier against his men. They didn't know he was behind him, and he looked around for a way to take advantage of this. A few feet away, he saw a gun. The General quietly moved over to it, picked it up, and crept behind the unsuspecting Sheriff.

"Drop your weapon," the General ordered, placing his gun against McCoo's head. "I would hate to leave a nasty hole in the back of your head. I am sure it could be quite painful."

Alex could feel the movement return to his arms and legs. An itchy, tingling feeling rose on his nerves. At the angle the General was standing, he thought he could reach his leg out from where Dogkey held him, kick out and knock the gun from the evil man's hands. It was worth a chance. With all of his focus and energy, he willed his leg to kick out, and it did. The toe of his bare foot connected with the gun's handle and sent it spiraling across the shaking laboratory.

"Well, uh, uh," the General stuttered, backing away. "I guess I will be going now."

"Do your worst, buddy. Make the general pay," said Alex, patting his mixed-breed friend.

Dogkey sat Alex down and rose in front of the General. He grabbed the terrified man by his shoulders and squeezed as hard as possible. The scar-faced General began to scream in extreme agony as the bones of his arms snapped above the elbows.

"Don't kill him," Alex pleaded. "Remember, it's wrong. But you can hurt him badly."

Dogkey thought about it. The man he held in his arms had tortured him, experimented on him, and caused him more pain than he cared to remember. Why shouldn't he kill him? The General deserved it, didn't he? But then he remembered what his friend had explained to him. His highly evolved mind had processed it, and it made sense. Not killing the evil man was the right thing to do. Releasing his tight grip, the General dropped a few feet to the ground and yelped in pain as his legs gave out, and he fell into a lump on the floor.

"How many other experiments are in here?" Alex asked, leaning over the dazed General. The General didn't respond. "I can always have Dogkey try to squeeze the information out of you."

"No, please," the General pleaded, scooting a few feet back. "I'll tell you what you want to know. Just keep that thing away from me."

"Answer the question, then," McCoo said over his shoulder, firing a few more bullets into the crowd of Agents still trying to make their way into the lab. For the first time, he noticed that blood didn't come out when the bullet hit the blue-suited men. Instead, some bright yellow liquid sprayed the wall. He knew they looked identical, but never questioned if their biology wasn't normal. They weren't human.

"All the rooms are empty except these. We have only a small number of experiments on the premises at this time." The General motioned to the eight doors off of the central lab.

"You're lying," Alex yelled. He finally had enough feeling in his legs to stand. "What are those rooms I saw when you dragged me in here."

"We haven't had a chance to fill them yet," the General responded, tears of pain forming in the corners of his eyes. "I swear. Keep that freak of creation away from me."

Dogkey growled and stepped forward.

"He understands your words," Alex commented. "I would suggest you don't upset him. He has a bad temper."

"I will cover you," McCoo said, firing a few more shots from the M-16. "Go open all the doors and move them down the corridor. I threw the first grenade down, it stayed clear of those blue-suited freaks, and there was an elevator at the end. You have to hurry. I'm almost out of ammunition."

Alex found his footing and was happy he could move again. He headed towards the first door.

CHAPTER FORTY

Alex opened the first door and was nearly run down by a creature that reminded him of something from mythology. It had the lower body of a horse, with four legs, and the upper body of a man. He couldn't remember what they were called but thought it started with a 'C.'

He moved on to the next door and flipped it open. Nothing moved or came rushing towards him, but something was in there. Several small clicking sounds echoed from the darkness. "You're free," Alex yelled into the black void. "You can come out. But hurry."

Suddenly, several small red eyes appeared, and Alex instantly recognized them. The room was filled with Shrats. He quickly closed the door and could hear their tiny bodies collide with the backside of the metal. Some creatures didn't deserve saving, he thought to himself. He re-locked the door and moved on. He didn't give the tiny monsters another thought.

"You have to hurry," Sheriff McCoo yelled, firing a few more shots at the Agents. "We need to go."

Alex didn't waste any more time examining the contents of each room. Instead, he rushed up to each door, unlocked it, and moved on to the next. Slowly, creatures of all shapes and sizes began to filter out. As Alex passed by each door, he motioned to them to head down the hallway.

Fighting to get out of the lab, the mixture of beasts trampled over the slower of them, trying to be the first to get out. Alex wondered why it was that he and Dogkey were able to form such a close bond. They had no regard or thoughts for their fellow captives. Maybe the two of them were better than the other creations or cared about others more than themselves.

With the last door opened, Alex rushed back to McCoo and Dogkey. "That's all of them."

"Good," the Sheriff replied. "Have Dogkey grab the general. We're getting out of here." The Sheriff pulled the pin of another grenade and threw it at the approaching Agents. An explosion followed, sending the duplicate men flying in all directions with splashes of the bright yellow liquid they had for blood. More of the roof came loose and smashed the machinery below it. The whole facility was coming apart.

The trio turned to leave but paused when they saw the General sitting up behind them with a gun in his hand. He could barely hold it up but attempted to point it in their direction. "No one takes from me. This is my lab, my work. You can't just come in here and do this."

Dogkey rushed forward. The General pulled the trigger of the handgun several times until the clicking of the chamber indicated he was out of bullets. Each round from the barrel of the gun collided with Dogkey's chest. Due to his weakness from the sun and the burns across his body, the bullets easily penetrated his skin and caused him to fall to the ground only a few feet from the General.

"No," Alex yelled, rushing to the side of his hairy friend. "I swear, you will pay for this."

Sheriff McCoo approached the general and struck him in the head with the butt of his rifle. The gun fell from the scared face man, and he fell back, dazed and confused. McCoo kicked the gun away and joined the crying Alex at the side of the mixed-breed monster lying motionless on the ground.

"Let's roll him over," McCoo said, pushing under the shoulder of the creature's left arm. They rolled Dogkey on his back, and the Sheriff could see his condition instantly. The blank stare from its open eyes looked off into the abyss. The soul was gone, and the brave creature was dead. He put his arm around the kid. "I'm sorry, he's dead."

Alex threw himself across the bloody chest of his friend. He cried harder than he had ever done before. Sheriff McCoo wanted to allow the boy to mourn, but they had no time.

"We have to go," McCoo said, dragging Alex off the lifeless body. "There isn't much time left."

Alex fought to get back to his friend, but the Sheriff was stronger and dragged him to the hallway that led to the elevator. They had just entered the corridor when the General launched himself onto Alex. The boy fell to the ground under the weight of the scar-faced man. With both arms broken, the General was not much of an adversary, and Alex could push him off him.

"You just don't give up, do you," Alex said, brushing the dirt from his clothes.

"You are mine," the General demanded through clenched teeth. "I won't let you take him."

"I would never want to be accused of taking something without paying for it. What kind of example would that set? How about if I leave something behind," Sheriff McCoo said sarcastically. He pulled the last grenade from his pocket, dislodged the pin, and dropped it beside the evil man on the ground. He grabbed Alex by the shirt, and both humans rushed down the corridor.

The general fumbled to stand and escape the grenade, but he was too hurt. The grenade flash was the last thing he saw as the weapon obliterated him. This final explosion was the last that the facility could take. The roof crumbled, and tons of dirt, rock, and cement rained down on the destroyed lab.

Sheriff McCoo and Alex had made it around the first bend in the hallway when the grenade went off. The pressure of the blast sent them tumbling forward in a cloud of dirt and rock. They picked themselves up without saying a word and continued towards the elevator. As they approached the final corner, dread spread across the Sheriff's frustrated face. The elevator had already started up the shaft. What were they going to do?

"How did they figure out to work it?" Sheriff McCoo asked, both surprised and frustrated.

"Just because they were experimented on doesn't mean they were stupid," Alex responded.

The destruction that had started burying the lab was moving up through the hallways. Sections of the hallway began to collapse. Soon, the whole facility would be buried.

"What are we going to do now?" McCoo asked.

"Look," Alex said, pointing to the carved-out section of the elevator shaft. "A ladder."

A wide ladder was embedded against the metal frame of the elevator shaft and two feet in. It was designed for someone to climb if the elevator broke or needed service.

"I guess we climb," McCoo added. "You go first."

Alex grabbed the rings of the ladder and began to climb. He looked back to where Dogkey had fallen and didn't see his body. It was probably all the debris and dirt cloud obscuring his vision, but the thought of this friend still alive was a pleasant thought. A thought he shook away and continued to climb. After he had made it a few yards ahead, Sheriff McCoo followed. They looked down as they climbed, surprised at how fast dirt and debris filled the hallway and the bottom section of the elevator shaft. This made the two survivors more eager to climb.

Halfway to the top, Alex and McCoo felt exhausted and out of energy. Both had different injuries that added to the difficulty, but sheer exhaustion threatened to stop their ascent. They paused to catch their breath, each aware of the problem of the other in continuing to climb.

"Uh-oh," Alex said, observing the elevator start to lower again. "We have a problem."

"What kind of problem?" the Sheriff asked, looking up past the boy. He saw the ascending elevator and quickly sucked his chest in. "Did anyone ever tell you that you have the gift of understatement? Squeeze in. Hopefully, there will be enough room for it to pass."

The elevator zoomed down. McCoo and Alex pushed against the wall as hard as they could. It passed Alex without a problem, but as it passed the Sheriff, a slight protruding hook snagged on his shirt and ripped it from his upper body with tremendous force.

Sheriff McCoo's grip became loose, and the strength of the shirt being pulled had yanked him backward. His hands slipped, and he fell down the elevator shaft. Luckily, the elevator had only lowered a few feet below, so McCoo was able to recover quickly as he landed on the lowering floor.

He walked across the descending floor and jumped for the ladder. Missing, he hit his head against the metal and fell back to the elevator floor. Rapidly standing, he moved back over to the ladder and jumped again. His right hand wrapped around the ladder ring while he inserted his other between the bars for a better grip. He steadied himself and began to climb back up towards Alex. With a newfound energy, he returned to his original position quickly.

"Are you okay?" Alex asked.

"I'm fine, but don't stop climbing. Things are going to get pretty hot around here."

"What do you mean?"

"Trust me."

The elevator floor collided with the rocks and dirt flowing into the shaft. The lift tried to lower, but its path was blocked by debris, and it couldn't reach the bottom floor. The motor driving the ride began to whine and squeal. Sparks flew from the sides of the engine casing at the bottom of the shaft, followed moments later by the entire engine exploding. Flames and metal parts were thrust up the elevator shaft by the force of the explosion.

"That's why," Sheriff McCoo yelled, pushing Alex further up the ladder. "Hurry. Climb."

Alex and the Sheriff climbed as quickly as they could. The feeling of possible death gave them a new sense of energy and drive. The flame chasing them up the shaft followed until the last second and died out as they reached the second to last floor. They could feel the heat of the explosion, but luckily, they were both unhurt. The flame died out.

Continuing to climb, they made it to the top of the ladder. With the floor at the bottom of the shaft, they wondered how they would reach the door. Their answer came as soon as they got to the upper room. The top of the ladder ended at a window to the left of the front door. Alex pushed it open and climbed out to the street above. The Sheriff soon followed. Exhausted beyond description, both survivors dropped to their butts on the wooden sidewalk.

"We made it," the Sheriff said, rubbing the sweat out of his eyes with the blistered palms of his red hands.

"Not all of us," Alex replied, sadly thinking about his friend buried below in the rubble.

"You were right, and I was wrong," Sheriff McCoo said. "He didn't kill that General. If he had, he would still be alive, but instead, he chose to do what was right, not what was natural to him. His only concern was to protect you. He was a hero in the end."

"He was a hero since he was created. It's just that no one could look past his appearance to see it."

"I did. And I am the first to admit I was wrong. He saved me when he didn't have to," Sheriff McCoo said.

Alex and the Sheriff sat silently and looked at the darkness around them. The street was quiet and empty.

"Hey, Sheriff." Alex turned his head towards the lawman.

"Yeah, kid."

"What happened to all those experiments I set free?"

"Not sure. I don't see any of them." Sheriff McCoo strained to look in the darkness. "The elevator came down empty, so we know they made it. My guess is they scattered into the night."

"I hope they weren't all sensitive to the sun. Otherwise, they are going to be in trouble soon."

"They couldn't all have been," the Sheriff imagined. "And those that did probably will find a hiding spot."

"Does that scare you?" Alex asked.

"Sort of. Especially with them being near my town. But I will tell you this much. I will not see them as the monster first. Who knows, maybe I might even be able to help a few of them?"

"There is a chance for you yet."

"Thanks, kid," the Sheriff replied, standing up. "But that's a problem for another day. Let's get you and me to the hospital." It took some time for McCoo to stand. Once on his feet, he helped Alex up, and they both shuffled to the car. The building behind them began to crumble and slip into the ground. The space that was in the lab was filled like a sinkhole with everything stacked above it. "I hope the car still works."

CHAPTER FORTY-ONE

"Are you ready," Sheriff McCoo asked, pulling the curtain to the hospital room aside.

"Just putting on my shoes," Alex replied, tying the laces of his new left shoe. "By the way, thanks for the clothes and shoes."

"No problem. I figure that after having to spend three days in the hospital. You deserved some new threads."

"I was wondering what it would feel like to wear shoes again. It will take a long time for my feet to heal."

"Other than that, how are you feeling?"

"Fine. The Doctor gave me a clean bill of health. I guess my system fought the high cholesterol as well. Good to know, I guess, when I am older and overweight. How about you? Feeling better?"

"I got fortunate. I am ready to return to work with the bullets passing through me and missing all my vital organs. A little sore in my muscles, but nothing to keep me from doing my job. Dogkey did a good job on his bandaging."

An awkward silence filled the room as Alex thought about the question he wanted to ask. He just wasn't sure he wanted to know the answer. But it would be hard for him to go on looking over his shoulder.

"Did they find the facility?" Alex asked.

"The real Feds are all over that place. But they are still digging. My guess is we won't know for a while what they find. They may call you in a few days to talk to you. Their supervisor is an Agent Trudy. Just in case you hear from them."

"That's fine," Alex responded sadly. "I just hope they find him."

"You have to face up to it. There is no way that Dogkey could have survived. He was dead. I saw him. You have to let it go. We both know he wouldn't want you to be sad."

"I know. I swear, when I looked back, he was gone." Alex tied his second shoe. "Have they found any of the experiments we let loose?"

"Not yet. They had trouble believing some of our descriptions, but I am sure they are looking anyway. They know something happened; they won't confirm what it was. One thing curious, though, when they searched the area, the Doc was gone. They are still looking for him, but something tells me he disappeared for good. Those secret government types are good at hiding away."

Alex finished tying his shoes and jumped off the edge of the bed. "So, how do I look?"

"You look ready to go home."

"Good."

"Have you thought about what you will say to your mother or Father" Sheriff McCoo asked, concern in his voice?

"Not yet, but it is a long drive to Duncan. I'm sure I will think of something to say."

"Maybe this will help her believe you." Sheriff McCoo handed Alex a three-inch sharp fingernail. It was white, with a bit of black on the tip.

"Is this what I think it is?"

"Yep, when Dogkey broke you out of my cell, he broke two nails on one of his hands. I gave one to the Feds to collaborate our story and figured you could use the other one with your mom."

"Thank you. I appreciate everything that you have done."

"It's no problem. If you want, when we get there, I can go in and talk with her. I can explain everything, and then you can come in. It might soften the blow or at least help ease her into it."

"I appreciate the offer, but my mom will only accept this if I walk up to the door and say hello."

" Okay, but I am here if you need me. Let's hit the road. It will be dark soon, and I don't like the dark."

"Me neither," Alex said. "Me neither."

CHAPTER FORTY-TWO

The anxious energy was palpable in Special Agent Brian Trudy. He stood at the edge of the small movie-set town with the wind playing through his deep black hair. He turned to face his partner, Agent Wertz, who approached with a solemn expression. "What have they found in the facility?" Trudy asked, dreading the answer.

Wertz cleared his throat, and nervousness was evident in his voice. "Exactly what we expected: dead staff and experiments—including all the clones in the Blue Agent project."

Trudy shook his head. "Not good. The Deputy Director won't be happy about this. What about the body of the General?"

"It was recovered an hour ago...sort of."

Confusion flashed across Trudy's face. "What do you mean, sort of? Either we have it, or we don't?"

"We haven't found all of him yet," the Agent reported. "It appears he was too close to a grenade when it went off."

Trudy shook his head in disbelief. "Do you have any good news for me?"

The Agent nodded. "Most of his notes were recovered, and so far, we've rounded up over fifty percent of the released creatures. They're en route to the new maximum-security facility in Montana via the General's Agent legion, and Doctor Williams has been informed about their arrival. We anticipate capturing the rest by tomorrow."

"Good," Trudy said. "What else?"

"Oh, and the Sheriff inadvertently gave us one of the creature's fingernails when pulled from one of the Blue Agents. I presume you want them to use that for cloning?"

"Of course. Please send it to Doctor Williams but remind them they can create DNA from something as small as a hair follicle. This fingernail may give them too much to work with."

Wertz nodded. "What about the boy? Are we to recapture him?"

Trudy paused before responding. "No, not at this time. Too many people know who he is now, even the local Sheriff. I've got other plans for him. The experiment never ended, and there are still more chromosomes to explore. We will just let things cool down a bit first. We have another facility to work with in the meantime."

Wertz's eyes widened. "How did you..."

Trudy smiled as he stared off into the darkness. "I know a great many things, Agent Wertz. Among those, your previous assignment." He held up his hand before Wertz could reply. "And I don't care. We need to move forward."

"Excuse me, sir." The shout came from a pop-up tent several feet away. "I think we have something."

Trudy and Wertz rushed over and entered the command center tent. Their eyes were glued to the three massive screens before them. The image was grainy and flickering, but the thermal picture was clear enough to make out the shape of a giant creature moving across the dark desert. It was twice the size of a man, with a thick hide that lowered its heat signature. However, there was still enough heat for it to show up.

"What is that?" Trudy asked.

"It appears to be subject 2341sa. Also called Dogkey."

"I was told it was dead."

"It was, sir, and I saw them load the creature myself."

"Get me the driver online."

The technician's hands ran across the keyboard and connected. A distraught voice came across the speaker. "Lorpe here. Can I call you back?"

Trudy spoke up. "This is Agent Trudy. No, you cannot. What is your status?"

"Sorry, sir." Lorpe cleared his throat. "We have a problem. One of the subjects in the truck woke up and ripped through the side of the truck. We have lost it."

"Find it," Trudy said, signaling the technician to end the call.

"Perhaps it also has the ability to regenerate like the boy," Wertz said quietly.

"What is the source of this image?" Trudy asked.

"We have a drone with thermal imaging scanning the nearby area. This is about two miles away."

"Any theories on where it's going?"

"It's headed directly south of our position. Beyond that, no idea."

The image disappeared on the screen.

"Where the hell did it go?"

"Sorry, sir. It may have found a way to cool its core temperature. It is designed to operate in a stealth mode."

Trudy stepped out of the tent, Wertz close behind.

"This whole operation is fubar'd," Wertz said.

Trudy stopped and spun around. His face was inches from Wertz. "No, shit. We need to fix this. We have a boy and now some monster out in the wild, and we can't touch either of them. We need to move quickly out of this region if we want to maintain the secrecy of this program."

CHAPTER
FORTY-THREE

Sheriff McCoo pulled his blue Toyota Sentra to a stop in front of the medium-sized adobe house in the suburbs of Duncan, California. He turned off the engine and twisted to stare at the young man sitting next to him. They sat silently until Alex reached out and turned the handle to the door. It swung open, but he didn't move. He just stared at the steps of the walkway.

"Sure, you don't want me to go with you," Sheriff McCoo asked. "I can explain what happened."

"No," Alex said, shaking his head. "I need to do this alone, but I appreciate it."

"No problem, kid."

Alex reached over and hugged McCoo. The Sheriff didn't know how to respond. He embraced the boy's back and patted him.

Alex stepped out of the car, his heart racing as he stared at the familiar yet strange front door. Taking a deep breath, he reached out and knocked hesitantly. He heard hurried steps, the deadbolt turning, and a click when the door opened.

His mother stood there in shock, her face drained of color. She had thought he was gone forever, yet here he was, standing in front of her--alive and well.

"Hi, Mom," Alex said with a timid smile. "We had a little trouble on the phone, so I decided to come home."

"But... you died," she stammered.

"You're right, I did," Alex replied, pausing to take another deep breath. "But I got better."

The two of them embraced as tears started streaming down their faces.

About The Author

Brian Daffern is a native of California and was born in San Diego. He currently resides in Georgia with his wife and 4 daughters. In addition to being an author, he is a well-educated Marine, a senior leader at a well-known technology company, and a member of the Scientific Coalition of UAP Studies.

Books By This Author

Prince Albert in a can

The Beast School

The Realm Pirates

Ambient Knight

The Gossamer Gambit

Alien-ated